A COLLE

WORKS

Short Stories

Excerpts

Poetry

Presentations

&

Father Pietro's Guide to Personal Peace

And Professional Success

Peter Rizzolo

Create Space, a division of Amazon Publishing

Cover Design by Joe Rizzolo and Ruth Eckles

Acknowledgments

I want to thank my writing group leader, the late Charlotte Hoffman, for her encouragement and insightful analysis of my writing. Other group members included Hal Glickman. Chuck Hauser, Beverly Lemons, Tom Shetley, Frank Stallone, and Fabienne Worth. Each contributed their unique perspectives and insights to my early drafts.

Dedication

This work is dedicated to my mother, my brother Tony, and my sisters: Helen, Geraldine, Phyllis, Chickey, Frances, my children, and my extended family.

Guy Heaven

I stepped from my car in the Lowes Home Improvement parking lot and took a deep exhilarating breath. The sun shone brightly, the sky an intense blue, the air celery crisp. As I approached the store entrance, a middle-aged black man dressed for work, carrying an eight-foot-long pressure-treated four-by-four, walked toward me. He was whistling *I'm Popeye the Sailor Man.* He acknowledged my smile with a nod but didn't miss a note of his bouncy melody as he walked briskly past. He was happy. He had just paid a visit to guy heaven.

The store's oversized automatic doors opened grandly as I entered. I grabbed a nearby lumber cart and soon realized why it was so readily available. It rose and fell with a loud irritating thump as I pushed it forward. Would it roll at all when piled high with lumber? Might I need the store's forklift to carry the entire cart to the checkout counter? I tried several carts before I found one with relatively round wheels.

I searched for nails before selecting the lumber section. I needed to repair my deck. Why I wondered, are the nails so far removed from the lumber section? Not wanting to clunk down several isles with my empty cart, I threw on several two-by-fours from a nearby bin and left the cart to rest for a while. I already had untold varieties of nails in my home workshop; roofing, serrated, galvanized, finishing, casement, and sheetrock nails, to name a few—all in various metals, sizes, and caliber. Still, one doesn't want to risk running out of nails in the middle of a project.

As I passed the cement, gravel, and insulation section, I thought about the concrete-like plaque that was undoubtedly accumulating in my coronary arteries even as I walked with brisk determination. What would it be like to have a heart attack in Lowes? Of the tens of thousands of items they carried, I bet there wasn't a single life-saving aspirin in the store. Gradually a group of middle-aged employees with bellies trussed in leather supports would form a circle around my prone body, shaking their heads and saying, "what a pity; he was such a good customer."

Would the store be my personal limbo? I could do worse. Such thinking was, of course, nonsense. Rescued by several surgeries and sustained by prescription drugs, I enjoy reasonably good health.

The tune, *Popeye the Sailor Man,* kept going through my head. I wish I could whistle like that fellow in the parking lot. My whistle is a sort of tonal hiss that issues forth from my parted but motionless lips.

Please excuse the detour. I was on my way to get my nails. Before I got there, a display caught my eye. A power nailer was on sale for only forty dollars. Nailers are usually over two hundred dollars! Oh, I see, it nails brads, those short wire-like nails without heads. Brads are helpful for small projects, like tacking up molding or making small picture frames. Probably a frivolous tool. Still, nailing a brad does represent a challenge. One chances a crunched digit or two to get started, especially in hardwood. Although reasonably dexterous, I have managed to strike my finger once or twice. I picked up the colorfully packaged box containing the power nailer and tucked it under my arm—no more hammered thumbs for me. But needless to say, a power nailer is not a tool to be used while your mind ponders the complexities of the human condition.

It was impossible to pass the hardwood section without a moment's pause. The smell of oak, mahogany, and walnut makes the fine hairs on my arms go from prone to erect. I fingered the smooth surface of a black walnut board. I would have gathered up several boards had I had my cart with me.

I'm not a wood snob. I love the smell of pine and appreciate how gracefully the soft wood yields to my not-so-sharp planes and chisels. It also accepts stains beautifully and looks good even with a nick or dent here and there.

On entering my workshop, a neighbor once told me I must own every tool known to man. That, of course, is utter nonsense. I don't own a table saw. I own a radial arm saw, a chop saw, a hand-held circular saw, and two hand saws: a hack saw, a coping saw, a reciprocating saw, a band saw, a fret saw, a miter saw, and a veneer saw. Still, there are times when what I need most is a table saw.

Averting my eyes from the awesome table saw display, I turned into the nail and fastener section. To my left are metal drawers compartmentalized to hold an astonishing array of washers, screws, nuts, and springs—items made of stainless steel, brass, Teflon, and rubber. And, of course, each item comes in a variety of sizes. I had the uneasy feeling that I'd remember some small specialty item I needed as soon as I got home. Oh well, I'll no doubt be back there tomorrow.

Let's see. I need five pounds of galvanized, three-and-a-half-inch nails. Should I use a serrated nail or one with spiral grooves? Or should I use screws? I decided to buy a box of each. I hurried back to the lumber section, avoiding, with some reluctance, looking at the enticing wrench sets on display along the central aisle.

Before returning to the lumber section, I checked the electrical department. Perhaps I can find a chime that plays *I'm Popeye the Sailor Man?*

THE MUSIC GOES DOWN AND AROUND

It would be bad enough if my thoughts were interrupted by a tune de jour, but even more surprising, songs I heard as a boy now seem to pop into my head at unexpected times. So please bear with me.

In my real life, I'm a people-type doctor, immersed in a range of life's dramas, from bunions, colicky babies, broken hearts, and sundry bad stuff to which our fragile bodies and souls succumb.

But in the early light hours, when the birds outside my window screech with joy in anticipation of a new day, I lay, reforming my dreams to make things turn out the way I want. If only I could write down the images, the feelings that surge through me. "Zippidy do da, zippidy day, wonderful feeling!"

Knock it off, Jim. What's happening to your brain? I find myself whistling these old-time songs like This is the Army, Mr. Jones. Can you believe that?

Now concentrate on something significant, like relationships, communication, and the environment.

"Some enchanted evening, you will find your true love...."

Okay, I've got it. Think of Joe and Grace Lyons. Hey, not shattering, but it's a start. We had a great week with them in the Bahamas last winter, and now they've written and want to go on a canal trip on a houseboat in Britain. I'm sure it'll rain every day, and mold will begin to grow under my fingernails.

"I've got you under my skin deep in my heart."

Well, what can I say? Grace thinks England is the greatest. Me, I need to see the sun at least once a week. And my wife, Adrian, has the most sensitive nose I have ever seen on a two-legged creature. Finding a suitable motel accommodation that passes her nose test is hard. There are entire countries her nose has ruled out. I'm afraid the British houseboat doesn't stand a chance.

"I'm gonna wash that man right out of my hair. I'm gonna wash that man right out of my hair."

I guess I'll wait until next week to write Joe. I don't want to hurt their feelings, but two weeks of watching C-Span is more appealing.

"Every time it rains, it rains, pennies from heaven. Don't you know each cloud contains pennies from heaven?"

Well, tonight was our spa night. You know, it's kind of crazy. I'm in there doing aerobic dancing with primarily ladies, and my wife's out there pumping iron with those mega-macho types.

"Here's looking at you, kid."

Hey, that's not from a song. But now, lines from old movies also keep going through my head. It's embarrassing because most of my friends haven't the foggiest idea what I'm talking about.

"I'm not out of order. You're out of order."

Today I observed a medical intern interview a young man. She had to tell him his recent HIV test was positive. I watched the interaction on closed circuit video with the patient's consent. She was sensitive and skillful beyond what I would expect from someone so early in her training.

Why are women so good at that sort of thing? We probably started the same, but through the ages, the good listener men probably got their heads beat in by clubs and spears.

Communicating is another thing women do better; the ladies are good at most things that don't rely on brute force. Please note this: I predict that there will be affirmative action hiring policies in the next century to help men compete with women.

"All of me, why not take all of me? Can't you see I'm no good without you?"

You've got to admit that I am sensitive. I've even been known to cry when the band plays the National Anthem at a baseball game. Adrian says that has nothing to do with patriotism. She says I'm just sad because I'm not playing first base.

Baseball is like religion. There are a few converts here and there, but it's mostly tradition. I don't know, and maybe it's genetic. Adrian hates baseball less than any other sport, so I don't know if she fits into the converted has a recessive baseball gene.

"Buy me some peanuts and cracker jacks. I don't care if I ever get back."

Today was a special day. I was off, not on call, and had absolutely nothing planned. My basement workshop, crammed with wood scraps and a catalog's worth of tools, seemed an inviting place to tinker while the rest of our family slept. I quietly opened the basement door when Adrian said from the bedroom, "What's on your agenda today, Jim?"

I suspect a wisp of musty-smelling air had swirled through the house as I opened the basement door. Saw dust diluted to one part per trillion is probably sufficiently concentrated to alert Adrian's nose.

"Honey, my day's a clean slate. What would *you* like to do?"

That afternoon Adrian, Tim, Judy, and I went to the planetarium for a photographic exhibit and stayed for a special children's program called Star Trek Chapel Hill. Our family is larger than average by modern standards, with 2.33 children. Tim, our oldest, is nine, Judy is six, and we expect our second son in about three months. We know it's a boy because Adrian said it smelled like a boy. When the doctor did the ultrasound, he said he couldn't see any boy-type parts, so he was pretty sure it was a girl. I doubted it. Adrian's sniffer is seldom wrong.

"Oh, what a wonderful feeling. Everything is going my way.

Tim is a great age for my ego. He's gotten interested in baseball and is amazed that his dad, a man of such advanced age, can still play ball reasonably well.

Running bases looks easy, but getting out of bed the following day is like coming attractions for what I'll look like in 2010.

"Yo, yo DiMaggio, we want you on our side."

You talk about a hard day at the office. This morning, they brought in a migrant worker who had chopped off half of his index finger in a slicing machine.

"It's too bad you didn't bring in the finger. I could have sewed that baby right back on."

His foreman, a short round man, grinned broadly, revealing a set of tobacco-stained, widely spaced teeth. He produced a handful of assorted items from his pocket, including a prune-colored thing with a nail on the end of it. I suspected the inside of his pocket was like a Noah's Ark of bacteria, not an ideal place to incubate his severed finger.

The injured man, who couldn't speak English, was also grinning at me, and I realized he had gotten the drift of the conversation. As grubby and smelly as he was, I had the urge to hug and comfort him. My off-hand remark had raised expectations way beyond what was possible.

Crouched over a not-high enough examination table, I reconnected the finger layer by layer for the next two hours until it looked pretty good, except for its purple color. On a scale of one to ten, the finger's chance of surviving was about a minus one hundred.

Mia culpa, mia culpa.

Adrian, Judy, Tim, and I are driving to Atlanta this weekend. We have box seats at a Braves game Sunday afternoon. Tim has been oiling up his glove for a week. Adrian has a college friend who lives in Atlanta. They'll hang out while I take the kids to the ballpark.

"Roll out the barrel; we'll have a barrel of fun."

Late yesterday afternoon, dark clouds gathered, and an angry August storm poured torrents of rain on our quiet neighborhood. Tim was riding his bike, returning from a friend's home, just a few blocks away. While turning a corner, the rear wheel skidded, and he slid into oncoming traffic. It's impossible to even think about the accident in any rational way. It merges into a blinding white light—a place where there is no time or orderly sequence of events. Only a chorus of grief-stricken faces, hushed voices, sleepless nights, and a grinding ache transformed my body so that I felt more like a paper mâché manikin than a man.

Anthology

A year has passed since the accident. Adrian found my journal tucked in my sock drawer and thought it would be a good idea if I started writing again. I said I would try.

The car that hit Tim had no time to stop. He had no identification, but the Emergency room nurse recognized him because I often brought him with me when I made weekend rounds. She called and said I must come to the Emergency Room, that Tim had been in a car accident. I called Adrian. We met at the hospital but a blur after that. Tim lay on a stretcher, the curtains drawn around the tiny cubicle. He appeared to be sleeping, but his face was ashen. The emergency room doctor said he was thrown twenty feet and landed on a stone wall, crushing several ribs on his left side. They said he died of massive internal bleeding from a ruptured spleen.

Our parish priest came and went; streams of friends stopped by. Hours passed, but we couldn't leave our son lying there. I don't remember how we got home.

The next day, Adrian and I went to the funeral home to pick out a casket. It was all like a dream, a horrible dream. I never thought of Tim as being small. He was just Tim. But looking at that tiny casket, I don't know what. Devastating is the only word that comes close.

Family flew in from all over, gathered about us from start to finish, but soon they were all gone. It was just me, Judy and

Adrian. We clung together; we cried, talked about Tim, looked at old pictures, and cried some more.

Family and friends were helpful this past year, but it was the pregnancy and birth of Joel that saved us. We take each day with the children as a gift that can be reclaimed anytime. I've gotten a little crazy, calling home twice daily to talk with Adrian and ask about the kids. She says we need to go for counseling, that I'm not giving the children enough slack. But I'm okay. It's just that nothing I used to do isn't much fun anymore. The days are still filled with everything we've always done, but everything now seems burdensome and oppressive. I'm okay with my patients. I can navigate their world without the anchor of grief that causes me to move through my private time in slow motion.

The other day I was sitting on the bed in Tim's room. Everything was the same as it was a year ago; neither of us could change anything. Judy walked in and sat next to me. I was holding Tim's baseball glove.

"Why are you crying, daddy?"

"I was just thinking how much I miss your brother, Tim."

"Is that why you always have a mad face?"

"I'm not mad, sweetheart." I tried hard to smile at her, but somehow my facial muscles had forgotten how.

"You got me, daddy, but I can't play baseball as good as Tim."

I lifted her onto my lap. Her eyes seemed bluer than I had ever noticed. I squeezed her harder than I should have and forced a funny sound from her chest. I recalled a game we would play when she and Tim were little. They would sing a song, and I would press up and down on their chest, and their voice would come out shaky.

"Judy, you can use Tim's old glove. Let me get my mitt, and we can play a little catch in the backyard."

I walked along with Adrian, Judy, and Joel in a secluded but beautiful wooded area. I had Joel on my back in one of those papoose-type things. Suddenly the quiet was shattered by the unmistakable howling of wolves. Everyone stopped and listened. We could hear the sounds of running feet, growing louder and louder. Adrian grabbed Judy's hand and shouted, "Run, Jim, this way."

But I was unable to move from the spot. Adrian raced back to where I was standing and grabbed Joel. She pulled at my shoulder. "Jim, for Godsakes, come with us."

I glanced about me and saw a semicircle of glinting teeth and flashing eyes staring at me. As they slowly drew closer, I finally turned and began to run in the direction Adrian had gone with the children. No matter how hard I strained, my legs could not carry me along fast enough to keep the wolves from gaining on me. Finally, I reached a high wall. Adrian and the children were sitting on top. Judy said calmly, "Climb up, daddy, climb up quickly. We can't wait anymore."

I jumped repeatedly, but I would miss Adrian's outstretched hand each time I fell to the ground. The wolves tightened their circle around me. I sat in bed screaming, "Don't leave without me!"

Adrian was holding me in her arms. "It's okay, Jim; you just had a bad dream."

Judy and I have been practicing almost every day. When she pulls her blond hair into her baseball cap, she looks so much like Timmy that it chokes off my breathing.

What she lacks in skill, she makes up in determination. Today I told her, "We need to get you a new glove. Tim's old glove is too big for you. You'll need a different glove if you want to play first base in Little League this year."

It was quiet at dinner tonight. I was pushing the food around my plate as though I were inspecting it for parasites. Adrian had made her mom's chili recipe, going light on the pepper. I usually added extra.

"Daddy," Judy said, "The Bulls are playing at home this week. Can we go see them Saturday?"

Tim and I often went to the Bulls games, and sometimes the whole family went. We hadn't been since Tim died. I wanted to take Judy to the game but was afraid that somehow it wouldn't be right without Tim being there.

"I don't know, sweetheart, maybe one of these days."

"You been saying that and saying that." She turned to Adrian, "Mommy, you take me. I can't wait anymore."

I wanted desperately to bang on the table and say, sure, let's all go. But for some reason, I just couldn't. No one spoke for a long time.

"Jim, I don't know what to cook anymore," Adrian said. "If you lose more weight, you'll have to use diaper pins to hold up your pants."

Sitting in his high chair between Adrian and me, Joel thought that was funny.

He squealed and said, "Da da pans, da pans." And at the same time, he brushed a dish full of chili onto my lap. I just sat there looking down at my lap. Then Judy and Adrian started to laugh. They were laughing so hard that tears were streaming down their faces. I hadn't heard that laughing at the dinner table in a long time. Joel was joyfully banging his plastic cup against the tray of his high chair, no doubt believing everyone was laughing at his little joke.

Something inside me seemed to split apart, like a levy giving way. I began laughing and crying. I stood, looking at my lap as the chili slowly dripped to the floor. Weakened from laughing, I dropped to my knees. Adrian went to the sink and retrieved a wet dishcloth. I didn't expect her to toss it to me, and it sailed past me, knocking over a water glass as it landed on the dining room table. That caused another round of laughter and tears.

As I gingerly eased myself back into my seat, Judy said, "What about the game, dad?"

I looked about the table, and everyone was looking at me expectantly. I could hear Judy's voice saying, "*come, daddy, we can't wait any longer.*"

"Sure, let's all go to the game." I turned to Adrian and smiled, "Sweetheart, pass the chili and pepper. I'm starved."

"God loves you, dear Mrs. Robinson, heaven saves a place for those who pray, yea, yea,

OKAY TEN MINUTES

Alfredo came to New Jersey in 1970 and opened a pizzeria in rural Hunterdon County. It was a tiny establishment in a strip mall with only six tables, a counter, and a small oven. He worked alone. He made his dough by hand, but as his business prospered, he bought equipment that could mix large batches of the ingredients that went into his secret recipe. He had to reduce the number of tables from six to four because his new oven took up so much space. But most of his business was take-out, so it didn't concern him.

As his business continued to grow, so apparently did the friable cholesterol plaque in his left main coronary artery. One evening after a particularly exhausting day at work, he rose from the dinner table, grasped his chest, and fell to the floor.

Alfredo's widow, Philomena, was left to care for a thriving business and three children under five.

Alfredo's kid brother, Mario, worked in a shoe factory in Milan, Italy. He operated a machine that punched holes in leather and automatically inserted tiny metal eyelets. He wasn't exactly enthralled with his profession, and when the call came from Philomena, he jumped at the chance.

"Ma dove vivo? No ho soldi. Mario said. (Where will I live? I have no money)

"La mia casa è la tua casa," Philomena said. (My house is your house)

So, Alfredo's Pizzeria remained open, and soon even the most discerning of Mario's customers could not tell the difference in the quality of Mario's pizzas compared to his brother's. Philomena had shared Alfredo's secret recipe with Mario, and she dealt with all the suppliers, so the quality of the ingredients and toppings remained unchanged. At first, Mario, who spoke no English, never answered the phone. But after several months, he learned enough to understand what the customer wanted but could not carry on a conversation. He listened patiently, then said, "Okay, ten minutes." It took twenty minutes to prepare and bake a pizza, but Mario allowed the customer a few minutes to get there. After a while, people began to refer to the pizzeria as *Okay, Ten Minutes* instead of *Alfredo's.*

The youngest of Philomena's children was confined to a playpen when she wasn't breastfeeding him in the kitchen area. Once in his playpen, his tummy full of warm mama milk, he beat happily on an empty pizza box with his tiny fists. The two and four-year-old children sat at an open table with their coloring books or raced about the store to their mother's chagrin and the customers' delight.

For six months, Mario slept on the couch as he made feeble efforts to find an apartment. Mario loved the children and liked being part of a family. At twenty-five, he lived in Italy with his parents, younger brother, and sister. It is better for Philomena to have a man in the house. He felt little pressure or inclination to leave.

He would blush with shame when he had thoughts of Philomena. He was captivated by her dark almond-shaped eyes, warm, kind smile, and tender way she caressed her children. Who would think she has three children? He would be annoyed and even become angry when the young male customers flirted with her.

He didn't understand exactly what they said but could tell by how they looked at her as she walked from their table. He felt he must protect her. He gave them bad looks and put less mozzarella and a little extra salt on their pizzas.

He was falling in love with Philomena. It was a sin. His brother was not yet a year dead. He took no more than glances, precious moments when he committed to memory every gesture, her smile, and even the funny way she held a pencil between her ring and middle finger. He loved it when she stood close to him as she gave him a customer's order. At times he'd feel the fiery touch of her thigh as she brushed past. He would quickly make a tiny sign of the cross on his forehead asking God to purify his thoughts. He bit his lip and twirled the pizza dough ever higher.

One night she turned toward him and smiled as she carried a pizza to a table. "Mario, you are in good form tonight. Osservate molto bello!" (You look very handsome)

As he thought about what she had said, he forgot about a revolving disk of dough that hovered above his head. Much to the customers and children's delight, like the Holy Spirit, it descended upon his head and shoulders. He laughed as he bunched the dough back into a ball. She thinks I am handsome. She smiles like an angel for me.

Philomena purchased a Berlitz's English Language book, and on Mondays, when the pizzeria was not very busy, she spent time teaching Mario English. She was surprised by how quickly he developed a feel for English grammar. Within a few months, he was able to carry on a halting conversation with their customers.

His sense of humor and playfulness delighted their customers. One young, beautiful college student was fond of pizza, or so it seemed, judging from how frequently she came to eat there. Her name was Kattie.

"Mario, Kattie likes you. Why do you ignore her? I see how she looks at you.

"She is too smart for me. Do you notice the books she reads?" Besides, someone else has my heart."

"I know how much you love Sophia Loren," she said. "Perhaps someday she will walk into our pizzeria."

Mario loved it when she teased him. "My love belongs to someone much closer."

She shook her head as the color rose in her cheeks. "You must not wait too long to tell her."

That night, as he did most every night, he arrived home exhausted. Philomena, as usual, had left early to get the children to bed. Mario flopped onto the living room couch and was soon asleep. His dreams were not of Italy or pizzas but always of Philomena. He could look into her eyes without guilt and repeatedly say, "Ti amo, ti amo."

Someone was shaking his shoulder, but he didn't want to let go of his dream. The gentle tugging persisted. Another customer, no doubt, Mario thought.

"Okay, ten minutes," he said, not fully awake.

"Mario," Philomena whispered.

He rolled over and was startled to see her kneeling beside him.

"You are so like your brother in many ways, ma lui besogno solo cinque minuti. (But he asked for only five minutes! Mario, ti amo. Vieni al letto." (Come to bed)

DANTE’S HELL REVISITED

When Dante Alighieri wrote The Divine Comedy, he was unaware of the full extent of man’s greed and how his ignorance would bring the world to the brink of destruction. Therefore, I humbly presumed to add to Dante’s third circle of hell where glutinous shades reside. A sub-section is reserved for those who flagrantly abused the environment.

Anthology

As Virgil and I, the gluttonous, did depart,
In the distance, there arose an acrid cloud that
Even from afar did cause mine eyes to smart.

"Through this perilous region, we must descend,"
He cried, "To reach the prodigal and the avaricious.
Shield thy face, or we must our path amend.

"Most odious fumes designed to fit their crime!"
We stood atop a narrow ridge that looked
Upon a massive lake of viscous bubbling brine.

In this barren domain, not a single tree or plants,
Did I see, except for mountains of man-made waste
Where legions of shades, like an army of ants

Labored feverishly to gather and transport
To the gaping mouths of three-headed ghouls
Garbage, glass, and plastic of every sort.

The refuse and shades they devoured pell-mell
And from their bowels, they soon disgorged,
Molten waste and dismembered shades as well

Peter Rizzolo

The arms, legs, and heads and beating hearts
Of shades slithered upon the slimy bank,
Desperate to rejoin their severed parts.

Once rejoined, the frantic shades writhed in pain,
Craving in vain but a single drop of water pure.
Unquenched thirst is their eternal domain.

Suddenly a cindered rain burned their eyes
Their writhing bodies, their muted agonized
Screams, their piteous silent cries.

"Who are these, master, who suffer thus below?
None do I recognize from my native land,
Or of whom through my broad knowledge know."

"They are from a time as yet to come to pass.
Their chariots of steel will need no horses,
Propelled by machines that drink a noxious gas.

"To increase the yield of crops for personal gain,
Fields were blanketed with man-wrought chemicals
That pollute the water and create an acid rain."

Anthology

“And in time, noxious gas filled the air above,
Glaciers melted, the sea rose, countless drowned,
A once pristine world no longer a place to love.”

The poet spoke of things man needed to thrive
That a loving God had provided for his people
From land and the sea, abundant food supply

Must my descendants face such unimaginable horror?
Destined to inhabit a world bereft of nature’s gifts?
My heart was near to bursting with this tale of sorrow.

Virgil, as though he had read my thought
Spoke softly as he hurried me along our journey,
Knowing this grotesque place had me distraught.

“He who gave man dominion over living things.
Those rooted in the soil, others that ambulate,
Creatures in the sea and those with wings.

“Though warned nature’s balance not be breeched
Man, consumed with greed, scoffing such admonitions
Ignored the cries of species that, for survival, screeched

"Greedy souls using resources to their own ends,
Continued to despoil the air and water, killing many
On whom the wellbeing and happiness of man depends.

"God aggrieved by what greedy creatures had begun,
Enlightened and inspired others with the wisdom
To gather the power of wind, water, and sun.

"Although the greedy had brought man's universe
To the brink of destruction, the balance of nature
Was by God and good persons in time reversed."

JUMPSTART

I waved to Frank as he moved gracefully into the center field position. Who would have guessed we were brothers? He's six feet two inches tall, has blue eyes and blond hair, and our mother's delicate features, whereas I'm a replica of my dad, five feet six, with dark brown hair and a nose that reflected my Roman ancestry.

The smell of hot dogs and roasted peanuts reminded me of the Sundays me and my brother had gone to the ballpark with our father. It has been over a year since dad died of lung cancer. How I wish he could be here beside me once again. He'd be so proud of Frank.

After the game, I put my arm on Frank's shoulder in the steamy locker room as he buttoned his shirt. "Not too shabby, two hits and two RBIs. Why not? Didn't I teach you the finer points of the game?"

Frank grinned. "Jeff Cummings will be coming with us… is that okay?" Frank asked.

The locker room was crowded with naked Carolina players shouting to one another. Jeff was on the trainer's table getting a rubdown.

"He looked pretty imposing on the mound," I said. "Is he a senior?"

"Yeah. Graduates in a few weeks. The team's going to miss him. Major league scouts have been sniffing around."

Although the restaurant was crowded and noisier than I would have liked, its polished mahogany bar, wood paneling, and brass footrail were appealing. I asked Jeff what he planned on doing after graduation.

"Carney Investors offered me a job as an account executive trainee in their Charlotte office. After a three months training program, they assign you a few accounts and guarantee a pretty good salary the first year."

"Frank tells me there've been some baseball scouts interested in you."

Jeff shrugged.

"Keep pitching like you did today," I said, "and they'll be waiting in line to sign you up. There was a time when I would have given anything for a chance to play professional ball."

Jeff stared at the highly polished mahogany tabletop. The beer bottle looked tiny in his right hand. I was curious why he would pass up a chance for a tryout with a major league club.

"Frank told me you're an artist," Jeff said.

"Artist in hiding. I earn my daily bread working for an advertising agency in Charlotte."

When he hesitated, I went back to baseball. "I still don't understand, Jeff...if I had pitched like you did today, my head would be as big as a watermelon."

Jeff shook his head, "Of the hitters, I faced today, how many you figure will make it to the majors?"

"Hardly any, but...."

"Exactly. When I come up against a strong hitter, I think, hell, in pro-ball, every hitter I face will be at least that good. I don't want to rot away on some minor league club living out of a suitcase for the next ten years. My dad's been pushing me to get an MBA degree."

"What the hell," Frank said. "As they say, an MBA in hand is worth two in the bush leagues."

I waved to the waiter to bring us another round of beer. "Jeff, if you decide to accept the job at Carney Investors, I'd be glad to have you stay with me until you find a place."

"Thanks for asking, but I wouldn't want to crowd you."

"I rent an old Victorian in downtown Charlotte. I have the entire first floor, and there's plenty of room for another person." I glanced at Frank and was relieved that he didn't say anything about Angela.

#

Frank called from Arizona. "We did it, big brother, NCAA. National Champs!"

"Mom and I saw the game on TV. We're proud, Frank. You played a great game."

"How about Jeff going the distance? And like you predicted, a scout for Atlanta approached Jeff after the game. He offered him a tryout for a Braves' farm club."

"Think he'll go for it?"

"He said he'd think about it."

A couple of weeks after graduation, Jeff called. "Hi, Paul, this is Jeff Cummings. Remember me?"

"Sure, congratulations on the championship. Are you still planning to move to Charlotte?"

"I've decided to take the job with Carney. I wonder if your offer's still good?"

"Sure, until you get settled, I'd be glad to put you up."

#

After Jeff moved into my apartment, he became interested in my artwork. I took him to a few exhibits and enjoyed explaining what I believed the artists were trying to express.

"It must be great to have something you're that excited about," Jeff said. "What time do you get up? You're already painting when I get up at seven."

"Around five, I can get in two or three hours before work."

"Ever think about showing your work?" Jeff asked.

"I'm not ready for that…another five years maybe. "

Jeff didn't say anything for quite a while. I knew what he was thinking: once I started making big bucks, it would be even harder to quit. Or maybe he thought he'd end up like me, hanging on to some job he hated, afraid to risk failing at what he wanted to do.

#

One evening toward the end of the three-month orientation at Carney Investors, Jeff came home, slammed the door, and walked into the kitchen where I was preparing dinner. He loosened his tie and sat at the table. "Damnit, I hate this job."

I walked to the refrigerator. "How about a cold beer?" I handed him one. I sat opposite him at the table.

He took a long drink. He stared off in space, lost in thought.

"My hearing's perfect, and my fees are reasonable."

Jeff went to the fridge, grabbed a bowl of left-over mashed potatoes, and sat at the table, scooping out globs with his index finger.

"I thought I'd be learning how to search out companies with growth or earning potential."

"Makes sense."

"But they have research specialists who do that. We get reports that read like sales pitches. The brokerage-house takes positions in certain firms, and then we're expected to recommend those stocks to our clients. No high pressure. Give them the facts." He went to the fridge and hauled out a bowl of leftover pasta.

"Is that legal?" I asked.

"As long as I inform them that CI has an interest in the company. And hell, the client figures if CI invested in the stock, they must believe it's a good prospect.

"Like selling cars," I said as I handed him a fork.

Jeff shook his head in disgust. "I can't decide whether to quit now or to stick it out for a year."

He stared at a nearby painting of a woman sitting in a field of wild flowers. "If I could paint like that…she's beautiful. Who is she?"

I wondered why he hadn't asked before. I picked up my empty beer bottle and began to peel off the label. I still felt like an empty silo whenever I thought of her. "That's Angela. We lived together for almost a year. She fell out of love a few months ago."

"Oh?"

"I've painted her so many times I can close my eyes and see her well enough to paint her again." By this time, I had the label completely off. I crunched it into a ball and tossed it in the kitchen sink. "I don't want to talk about it."

"Hey, my hearings good, and my fees are reasonable."

#

I knew something big was up when Jack Gibson, president of Gibson, Gibson, and Flint, asked me to meet with all three partners.

"Paul, our firm's been invited to submit a competitive proposal for an account many times larger than anything we have ever handled." He looked about the table. "We've decided that if we land this account, we'll make you a junior partner, with full partnership in three years." He took a deep drag on his cigar, then glanced at his partners, who nodded their heads like those little dolls people hang in their cars.

"No five-year phase-in," Joe continued, "no buy-in expenses..." He leaned forward and said slowly, "Only one string attached, Paul; we gotta catch this fish."

I was stunned. I looked at the other partners. They sat smiling and nodding.

"That's an amazing offer," I said. "This must be a hell of a big fish."

Joe Flint raised his bushy eyebrows for emphasis, "Not any old fish...we're talking, Moby fucking Dick."

"Moby Fucking Dick Industries? Never heard of them."

"That's what I like about you, Paul. You got a sense of humor. Have you ever heard of Vanguard Industries?"

"The tobacco conglomerate?"

He nodded. I was glad I had slipped on my blazer; my armpits were soaked. There was an uncomfortable silence.

Jack took a deep drag from his cigar, then exhaled a dense bluish cloud that hung over the conference table.

"Paul, the cigarette industry is hurting in the domestic market. They need to change their image. They've about given up on people over 40. They want to go after younger smokers. And they're not just talking about the domestic market. They believe their future is in Latin America and Asia."

I had the urge to tell them to go to hell and quit on the spot. "I have a real problem pushing cigarettes on young people. Could I have some time to think this over?"

Jack's face reddened. "Paul, this is strictly business. Big business. You have till tomorrow morning. Don't disappoint me."

That evening was Jeff's turn to cook dinner. I sat at the kitchen table, watching him chop onions, garlic, and fresh basil. I wondered how Jeff would have responded to the scene in the boardroom. I had thrown them a fadeaway curve ball, but Jeff would have fired a fastball right down the middle. I told Jeff about the conversation in the boardroom.

"Bastards. They know about your dad?"

"Sure, that's why they were nervous about asking me."

"You told them to go to hell?"

"God, I wanted to, but I can't afford to lose my job. So, I said I'd come up with a few ideas. Figure I'll hand in a proposal that looks good but won't be good enough to come out on top. That way, I keep my job, but the firm loses their bid for the contract."

Jeff didn't say anything, but the look he gave me made me feel like one of those gloppy messes my neighbor's dog deposits in front of my mailbox each morning.

Jack Flint personally supervised my progress on the bid for the Vanguard account. I presented several ideas at our second meeting. After studying them, Jack pounded the table.

"Paul, none of these proposals will fly, and you should damn well know it. You give me much better than this, or I'm subcontracting the job. I'm very disappointed, Paul, very disappointed."

I had underestimated Jack and realized I had to develop something better. Finally, I hit on an idea I thought would appeal to Jack. Rather than try to distract smokers from reading the small warning box, I decided to deal with the health risks head-on. I proposed to show young people involved in high-risk activities such as skiing, sky diving, and scuba diving. The ad would say, "Sure, there's some health risk involved in smoking. Look at the box! But it's not as risky as this...." Then under the photograph, the caption, "You can play it safe in life or go for the gusto. The choice is yours."

After I made my presentation to Jack, there was an interminable silence. I was ready to pass out from cigar smoke. He stood, resting both hands on the conference room table, "Son of a bitch, I think you've hit on something here. It's like saying, you're chicken if you don't smoke. Give me more variations on the theme, like kids skateboarding, water skiing, and maybe a motorcycle jump. I love the idea the more I think of it. This has to be top secret. We'll call a meeting of the entire staff. We'll promise fat bonuses for everyone if we land the account. We must have everyone's loyalty."

That night I told Jeff what had happened. "I couldn't believe how excited he was. He was practically bouncing off the walls."

"You hit a home run when all you wanted to do was get out of the way of the ball," Jeff said.

Sinking into my favorite chair, I leaned my head against the cushion, closed my eyes, and let out a massive sigh. "Maybe Vanguard will be scared off by the idea. After all, it does focus on the risks of smoking. They don't want that."

During the three-month training period at Carney Investors, Jeff would often be despondent and describe yet another way for an intelligent broker to transfer money from a client's account to his own. The worst part was that everything he had learned was technically legal. There were margin accounts, puts and calls, buying long, selling short, stock options, and commodity trading.

"It's like playing blackjack," Jeff said. "The odds are clearly in the house's favor."

"Why don't you quit if you hate it so much? I'm sick of listening to you beat your chest, stamp your feet, and then go back to work the next day. You hate yourself for not jumping when you had a chance to play with the Braves."

"I could say the same thing about you. You could have stood up to those guys at work. But you're too scared to give up a chance to become a partner. You caved, Paul."

I knew he was right. It was like a duel where each antagonist spun around simultaneously and fired into the other's chest. There was a long silence.

"I'm going for a walk, maybe take in a movie," Jeff said.

After work, one week later, I noticed a bottle of champagne on the kitchen table. "What are we celebrating?" I asked.

"I quit CI today," Jeff shouted from the living room

"You did?"

"And I called the scout for the Braves. He said they're still interested." He walked into the kitchen.

I threw both arms in the air. "Mama Mia, that is great news. Let's polish off the champagne, then I'm taking you out to dinner."

At the restaurant, we talked about Jeff's plans. He would move to Charlottesville, where the Braves have a Triple-A farm club. But mostly, he would be living out of a suitcase, traveling around the southeast. There was no bonus or guarantee of a contract. After the season, they would make him an offer if they liked what they saw.

"Paul, you've been working late almost every night. When do you guys bid on the Vanguard account?"

"Our proposal goes in next week. We should hear by the end of the month. After the first cut, there'll be two or three agencies left. Then they'll want variations on the proposal to ensure enough depth to support a long campaign."

"You're talking as though you want to land this account. I don't get it."

"I don't have any other choice. I made a mistake thinking I could get away with tanking it. And anyway, the idea is so straightforward someone else was bound to come up with it."

Jeff didn't say anything. He sat staring at his empty glass.

I poured us both more Chianti. How could I explain to him what had happened? "I got caught up in the whole competitive frenzy at the office. If this goes through, I stand to earn $200,000 in the first year. I can save a bundle in just a couple of years."

Jeff threw his napkin on his plate. "Damn it, I don't even know you anymore. All those talks we had about art. I guess that was just bullshit."

I pushed my chair back and signaled to the waiter. "I thought this was going to be a celebration. It feels more like 'the sermon on the mount.''

We had driven to the restaurant in my car. After paying the waiter, I tossed a five-dollar bill on the table. "I have to stop by the office. I hope you don't mind taking a cab back to the apartment. I'll see you later." I didn't wait for an answer.

When I returned to the apartment, I parked the car and went for a walk. I wasn't ready to face Jeff. I needed to think. I had talked with Jeff about my family and how my dad told me that when someone is given a special talent, like my ability to paint, it should be used for some good purpose. I still believed that, but the prospect of all that money was impossible to resist. Could I give up a prize that was within my grasp? A chance to retire early and devote all my efforts to my painting?

#

Two weeks later, Jeff was preparing to leave for Charlottesville. He had already loaded most of his things into his car. We hadn't spoken about the Vanguard account for the past few days. When he did ask, I said, "We made the first cut. It's down to one other agency and us."

He shrugged without looking at me, removed a dresser drawer, bumped its contents into a suitcase, and snapped it shut.

"I have an idea," I said, "how I might be able to come out of this mess with my self-respect intact. I'll write and tell you about it."

"Yeah," he said, "I hope things work out for you." He looked about the room. "I guess that's about everything." He walked over to me and reached out his hand. "And thanks for putting up with me."

Two months later, I mailed the following letter:

Oct. 31, 1998

Dear Jeff,

Gibson, Gibson, and Flint have a new client, Vanguard Industries. In just three months, we begin to test market the ad campaign. If all goes well, there will be a national blitz within six months.

About a year ago, a Seattle-based group called Concerned Americans contacted me about another matter. Their executive director said that they were getting hundreds of complaints about one of our ad campaigns. She came to Charlotte and met with Joe Flint. I sat in on the meeting. I admired her feistiness and noted that she was beautiful from an artist's standpoint. She said they would take Gibson, Gibson, and Flint to court unless we withdrew the ads. On the advice of our attorneys, Joe Flint reluctantly agreed to make some changes to the ad campaign.

I recently called her and, without identifying myself, explained that I had confidential information about a soon-to-be-released national cigarette advertising campaign that I believed to be unethical. She agreed to meet with me in Kansas City. At the meeting, I described the upcoming promotional campaign and showed her mock-ups of several of the ads. She was furious and concerned that it could be a very effective strategy. At first, she speculated that her group might try to get an injunction to prevent Vanguard from launching the campaign. I suggested that a counter-advertising campaign, playing on the risk theme, might be more effective. I mentioned to her an Atlanta-based non-profit group that produces anti-smoking posters to counter the glamour image the cigarette industry tries to project. I suggested that Concerned Americans might be able to convince them to launch an anti-smoking campaign with a theme identical to theirs but with radically different objectives. The ad could start: "Sure, cigarette smoking carries some health risks. Call up this gentleman. He'll tell you about it." The photographs would show sick-looking persons in wheelchairs, in intensive care units, carrying portable oxygen, etc., all with a cigarette dangling from the corner of their mouths. Underneath the following caption: "They went for the gusto."

Although she had guaranteed me anonymity, I wasn't going to risk being identified. I wore fake bushy eyebrows, horn-rim glasses, a three-day beard growth, and a blond wig to meet her. My mother would not have recognized me. The only thing that was not fake was the stack of ads I had brought with me.

She told me that Concerned Americans do not have the resources to match a giant conglomerate on a national advertising blitz, but there were other approaches they could take. I was told they have a sympathetic editor of a national weekly news magazine. She would push hard for a cover story. That would be picked up by the other newsweeklies, television, and hopefully, the talk shows. The anti-smoking ads could get millions of dollars of free exposure through the news media.

For now, I'll just mind my own business and quietly resign in a few months.

After you read this letter, please destroy it.

Your

friend, Paul

PS: At the end of our meeting, Ms. Baker said, "I liked you better as a brunette, Paul. But the eyebrows are a nice touch. If you shave, I'll even let you take me to dinner."

A FAMILY ODYSSEY

Summer of 1965

Alyce and I needed a break and were looking forward to a camping trip through the New England States. The open road, fresh mountain breezes, pristine lakes, quaint oceanfront villages, and the majestic sea beckoned us north. And as always, the last day before vacation was crammed with a demanding patient schedule and the ever-nagging telephone. Our oldest child, Geri, was nine, and the youngest, Jon, was almost three. All seven of us could fit, with a little determination, into the tepee-style pop-up tent that we used on weekend camping trips at the Jersey shore. But on this vacation, we were going in style. I rented a camping trailer that was sitting in our backyard, waiting to be tethered to our Chevrolet Impala station wagon.

The salesman at the dealership where I rented the trailer gave me a quick rundown on operating everything. "You're going to love this here baby. She's only a year old and still smells like new." As we circled the trailer, the salesman added, "Not a scratch on her."

It was almost twenty feet long and had a gas-operated stove and refrigerator and a 30-gallon pressurized water tank. There was a small bathroom with a shower. The salesman gave me a packet of instructions. The evening before our planned departure, after all the children had gone to bed, I sat at the dining room table with a map of the New England States. We planned to drive through New York, Connecticut, Massachusetts, Vermont, Maine, and New Hampshire. We planned on returning via New York to the Delaware Water Gap and back to Flemington. We would average about two hundred miles a day.

Alyce sat next to me, beads of perspiration gathering on her forehead, chewing absentmindedly on the end of a pencil. Her blue eyes, delicately sculpted features and wonderfully open smile could still make me feel mushy inside.

"What's the matter? Are you getting cold feet about the trip or just hungry?"

"What if we have car trouble, one day off schedule, and all our campsite reservations will be kaput."

I didn't look up from the map, tracing a yellow marking pencil along our planned route. "There are hundreds of campsites through New England. We can call around. Half the fun is not knowing how things will turn out."

She placed her arm around my shoulder as I continued to study the map, jotting down in the margins the time it would take between stops. I realized she needed this break even more than I did. She had worked as a nurse before the children started to roll off the assembly line, but now she was a full-time-and-a-half mom. The last time she visited her mother for a long weekend, she took our youngest child with her, and I played single parent. When she returned, the house looked like an army of crazed little people had invaded it. I can't say I didn't have fun with the children, but the days just weren't long enough to include cleaning up the place and doing the wash. Somehow Alyce got it all done. She has a mamma bear's energy and a mountain stream's tranquility. With six children to care for, there were occasional exceptions.

Our three-story Victorian house wasn't air-conditioned, and that summer had been a run-of-the-mill New Jersey high temperature, high humidity double whammy. We were looking forward to cool nights in Vermont and Maine.

The evening before, Alyce and I had helped the children pack their things. The reject pile included a box of comic books, a quart jug full of pennies, a pair of ski boots, an old 12" black and white TV set, a pet guinea pig, complete with cage, and enough food for about a month.

Peter, who would turn nine before returning from vacation, hung by one arm from a rung of an indoor jungle gym. "Dad, you always watch the news at night. Why can't we take the

TV?" He then swung onto a cross-bar and began scratching himself like a monkey. Joe, our second oldest son, who often took his queues from his older brother, began to squeal, bouncing about the room in a squatting position and chattering his teeth.

“It's thoughtful of you, Peter, to want to make sure dad doesn't miss his news programs," Alyce said.

"I can listen to the news on the car radio. The TV stays home."

I was the first to get up the following day. I shouted from room to room, "Hit the deck, mates. We're leaving at 0800 sharp. Bring your stuff out to the trailer."

It took almost two hours before all the food, clothes, camping gear, bedding, books, games, cameras, and who knows what else was loaded in the trailer. Everyone piled into the station wagon. I checked the trailer hitch and coupled the wiring from our station wagon to the trailer's electrical system.

I then began to back the trailer up our curved drive, bordered by a stone wall on the house side and large privet hedges along our neighbor's side. I'd never backed up a large trailer and was surprised to find how difficult it was. I attempted to back out, but the car and trailer would form a sharp angle each time. I had to drive back down the drive to realign the car and trailer. I finally began getting the technique and slowly advanced half-way up the driveway. As I picked up speed, Joe yelled, "Dad, you're headed for the hedges again."

I turned the wheel too sharply in the opposite direction, and the trailer drove forcefully into the stone wall. The sound of crunching metal and shattering glass filled the morning stillness. I got out and surveyed the damage. Alyce joined me. The left rear bumper was pressed against the corner of the trailer, scrunching in a section of paneling. The brake light was shattered.

The noise awakened Geri's friend Patricia, whose bedroom looked out the driveway side of their house. She raised her window and leaned out to see what had happened.

Geri rolled down the car window and shouted to Patricia, "Dad can't get the trailer out of the driveway."

"Okay, okay," I said, "no big deal, we can stop at Carver's on the way out of town and have them put in a new brake light." I had a sinking feeling as I realized I'd forgotten to check to see if my car insurance would cover trailer damage. I backed down the drive and unhooked the trailer from the station wagon. I then turned the car around, so it faced up the drive. Taking a heavy rope from the car trunk, I tied it to the trailer hitch and tied the other end to my rear car bumper. As I slowly drove the car ahead. The trailer was dragged around so it also faced up the drive. I then reconnected the trailer hitch to the station wagon.

"A little Yankee ingenuity, and we'll be on our way in no time"

"Will we have to do that every time we need to backup, dad?" Joe asked.

I gave him a withering look but didn't respond because I wasn't sure myself. As we drove down Main Street toward Carver's garage, a police car pulled up, lights flashing.

It was an officer I'd seen about town. He shook his head, "You got no brake lights on that trailer, Doctor Pete. I'm afraid I'll have to ticket you for that."

"I just busted the left light. I'm on my way to Carver's to get it repaired. The other light should be working."

"Neither is working, Sir. Come see for yourself."

I stepped out of the car and walked to the rear of the trailer. I shouted, "Step on the brake, Alyce."

"I don't understand. I checked it before we left."

I suddenly realized I had forgotten to reconnect the electrical cable that connected the car's brake light to the trailer when I turned the car around. The officer bent over and plugged the two wires together. "You see, it isn't too complicated."

I could imagine that little scene being repeated all over town. The officer could not suppress a slight smile as he wrote the summons.

When we finally left Carver's garage, it was 1:30 PM, and the thermometer at the Flemington National Bank read 87 degrees. Mark said he was hungry and thirsty. Soon everyone was asking to stop to eat somewhere.

"Give me a break, guys, we've been at it seven hours, and we're still only three blocks from home." I looked at Alyce for support.

“Why not pull over, Pete? We've got plenty of food in the trailer. We can make some sandwiches and be on our way in just a few minutes.

"The temperature in the trailer is probably well over 100 degrees. "Let's open the trailer windows so it can cool off while we drive," I suggested.

Soon, we were cruising along the highway with full bellies and empty bladders. Everyone was in a good mood. By late afternoon we crossed the George Washington bridge. Mark started singing, "The causeway, the causeway."

Geri interrupted, "This isn't the causeway. That's at the beach."

Joe wasn't impressed with that fine distinction. "It looks like a causeway to me."

"Yea, me too," Peter added. Soon all the children were shouting, "The causeway, the causeway."

On long drives to the beach, the causeway meant that we were almost there. It was a family tradition to express their joy on arriving.

"Pete, let's stop, I need some sunscreen, and the children could stand a break from the driving."

Turning off the highway at the next exit, I pulled to a curb to study the map. Geri, flipping through the trailer instruction book, said, "Dad, they say you're not supposed to leave those louvered windows open while the trailer is moving."

"It'll be hot as a sauna in there if we keep it sealed up all day. We can close then as soon as it cools down."

As I eased the trailer into traffic, the sound of crunching metal and shattering glass struck again.

"What was that?" Alyce asked.

I pulled over to the curb and hopped out of the car. There were fragments of glass and the remains of the trailer's window frames and screens all over the sidewalk. Alyce holding Jon in her arms, stepped out onto the sidewalk. She looked at the side of the trailer. "Oh my God, how did that happen?"

Four opened louvered windows were sheared from the trailer. I stood staring at the gaping holes in the side of the trailer. Looking along the curb, I realized what had happened: When I pulled up to look at the map, the trailer, slightly wider than our station wagon, overhung the curb. As we moved forward to leave, a telephone pole close to the curb had sheared off the windows.

"Oh Pete, how will we keep out the mosquitoes?"

"We haven't even gotten to the first fucking campsite, and look at the trailer!" I said in frustration.

They rarely heard either of us swear and never the "f" word. Geri had rolled down the car window. The children were stunned into a rare silence.

As Alyce and I walked back to the car, I heard Geri whisper, "Daddy's really mad. You'd better not say anything."

As we started to pull away, Mark asked, "Where are we going now, daddy?"

Three-year-old Jon, who had been privy to the street scene, turned his cherub-like face to the car's rear and announced proudly, "We goin' to the fukin camp."

Having camped along the New Jersey shore, we all knew that the dreaded monster mosquitoes would descend on us at sunset, attacking every inch of exposed skin. There was no reason to believe Connecticut would be any different. We stopped and bought screening, masking tape, a pair of hand shears, and a yardstick. Alyce measured and cut up the screening, and I taped it over the two gaping holes in the side of the trailer.

It was getting dark when I spotted the trailer-park sign just North of Old Saybrook. I reached over and squeezed Alyce's hand, "It's been one hell of a day, but I feel everything is going to be great from now on."

After traveling a few hundred yards, we pulled to a cabin marked "office." There, a woman gave Alyce a map of the campsite. "

We got the last available campsite. Much to everyone's surprise, I backed into the space with ease. It was already dark. We piled into the trailer and were soon asleep. "Where's Peter I asked as I snapped this photo the following day.

Joe shouted, "He's down there."

We discovered I had backed close to a low stone wall that separated the site from a deep gorge. We rushed to the edge of the wall.

Peter had climbed part way down the gorge, a rushing river at the bottom. It was a beautiful but terrifying scene.

"Peter, my God, be careful," Alyce shouted.

He was about 150 feet below us but far from the water, where the gorge's walls became much steeper.

"Don't dare go any farther down," I insisted. Come back up slowly. Watch your footing."

“It’s not that hard, dad,” Peter said as he made his way up without a hitch.

The following evening, we arrived at the second campsite we had reserved. We turned onto a narrow-rutted dirt road. Even at a snail's pace, the car and trailer shuddered whenever we traversed a deep rut. When we settled into our campsite, Joe was first out of the car, rushing to the trailer to use the bathroom. He shouted, "Dad, there's a flood in here."

Alyce and I stepped into the trailer. The refrigerator door was open, and a burst carton of milk lay on the floor. A dozen eggs, a broken jar of mayonnaise, and a carton of orange juice had also spilled from to refrigerator.

I assumed the refrigerator door must have swung open when we hit a rut.

"Daddy, the book said to be sure to snap the refrigerator door shut tightly, or it might bounce open," Geri said.

"Well, we had better make sure it's closed tightly after this, but for now, let's clean up this mess,” Alyce said. “And when we're finished, daddy's taking us all out to dinner."

After we loaded what could be saved back into the refrigerator, I discovered that the refrigerator door catch would not hold shut. I used several strips of masking tape to keep the door closed.

"Whoever goes into the fridge must re-tape the door shut afterward," Alyce announced.

The following morning Alyce got up at 5:30 and rushed to the bathroom. I'm a light sleeper and was awakened by the relatively quiet sound of her vomiting. I'd heard it many times through five pregnancies. No, it can't be, I thought. Maybe she's just car sick.

"Are you okay?" I shouted through the bathroom door.

"Sure, Pete, I'm doing my morning retching exercises."

Alyce came out of the bathroom. "My period is five weeks late. I was going to tell you, but I didn't want to ruin the vacation for you and the kids."

We embraced. Alyce's cheek was wet against my unshaven face.

"Pete, I'm not sure I can handle another child."

I felt sick. We had tried so hard after our fifth child four years. ago. The rhythm system had once again failed.

"It's going to be a girl, Pete. I just know it."

We stood there clinging to each other for a long time. I was calculating just how many years it was to menopause.

From Old Saybrook we drove past New London, where we picked up route 395 North, and we crossed into Massachusetts by mid-afternoon. As we headed up a steep hill south of Worcester, I noticed that the car was losing power. Despite the engine racing, we slowly came to a complete stop and then began to roll backward down the hill. As I scanned my rear-view mirror for any oncoming cars, I pumped the brake to slow us down. No one approached us from behind, but they would have little time to stop if a car or truck came over the hill. I slowly steered the trailer onto the shoulder, but the trailer extended a foot or two onto the road. A passing driver leaned on his horn until he was well out of sight.

"My God, Pete, this is dangerous. We have to get the children out of the car.

There was a smell of burning oil or rubber.

“Is the car going to catch fire?” Geri asked.

"No, I think the transmission is shot."

"Who got shot?" Mark asked.

"No one was shot. There's something wrong with the car, and we must get it towed to a garage. There's a house up ahead across the road. Let’s head there and call for help."

A man dressed in bib overalls answered the door.

"I'm sorry to bother you, Sir, but we're having car trouble. I wonder if I could use your phone to call for help?"

He looked past me, Alyce holding Jon, and the other four children huddled around her.

"Who is it, Jessie?" a woman's voice called from another room.

"Nearest garage would be in Boylston. It being Sunday, it's likely as not they won't be answering the phone,” Jessie said.

"I noticed a pickup truck in your driveway. Could you pull us to a place where the shoulder is wider?" I asked.

By this time, the man's wife came into the room, "Now, Jessie, don't you dare try to pull that trailer." Turning toward me, she continued, "He had a heart attack and isn't supposed to do anything strenuous."

"Come with me," Jessie said, moving toward the door. "Your wife and children can stay here. I can tow you to a rest stop about a quarter-mile up the road."

"Don't you fret, Jessie. I'm not going to pull that trailer with my teeth. I'll be just fine."

He had no problem towing the station wagon and trailer to the rest stop. He then drove back to the house to pick up Alyce and the children. On the way to the rest stop, Alyce, Mark, and Jon sat in the truck's cab. The older children and I jumped into the back.

The rest stop had clean bathrooms, food vending machines filled with unhealthy treats, sandwiches, soda, and a pretty elegant play area. The children were having a great time, and Alyce was happy not to be vomiting. I wondered if a lazy vacation at Long Beach Island, New Jersey, might have been a better choice.

The following day a tow truck from Boylston arrived to haul our car to a garage. He disconnected the trailer.

I drove to Boylston with the tow truck driver.

"How far are we from town, I asked.

"About three miles."

After checking the station wagon, the mechanic came to the small waiting area. As he rubbed his greasy hands with a not too clean cloth, he said, "You burned out your clutch Mister.

You need a heavy-duty clutch to haul that sized trailer up these hills. We're going have to get one from Worcester."

I wondered why the salesman hadn't told me I needed a heavy-duty clutch to haul the trailer.

"How long will that take?"

"Probably get one here by tomorrow, maybe the next day.

I decided to walk back to the rest area. We spent the next three nights in our trailer at the rest stop waiting for the car to be fixed. During the day, we packed picnic lunches and hiked through the countryside. It was all private property, but the people were friendly, often inviting us into their homes and giving the children cookies and milk.

On the second day, as we were hiking along a cow path through a freshly plowed and fertilized field, the sky darkened, and soon a heavy downpour drenched us and turned the trail and area into a muddy mess. As we headed down a gentle hill, Joe, who was in the lead, ran ahead, sat, and slid 30 to 40 feet before stopping at the bottom. Peter and Geri followed his lead. I handed Jon to Alyce and ran toward the crest of the hill.

"No, Pete, don't," Alyce shouted.

Bending into a ski-jumper crouch, expecting to descend gracefully down the muddy incline on my feet, I pushed off the edge. But instead of gliding, my feet sunk into the mud, and I catapulted forward, doing a belly flop into the heavily manure-scented soil. The children piled on top of me, and soon, we were all rolling around on the ground. Everyone but Alyce and Jon was having a grand time. She shook her head, thinking *I have five boys, not four.*

The rain stopped as quickly as it had started. By the time we reached the trailer, the hot August sun had caused the mud to begin to cake on our clothes and bodies. It took us hours to clean up the children. The pungent odor of manure lingered in the trailer for days.

By noon the next day, we were on the road headed for Milford, Vermont, expecting to arrive by late afternoon. The rolling countryside, with sparsely peopled farms, spread before us, a massive patchwork of undulating greens interspersed with furrowed rows of moist black soil.

Sitting next to me with a map spread on her lap, Alyce said, “There’s a lake just south of Milford. Let’s stop there before we head for the campsite."

Mark poked his head over the front seat, "Can I see mom?"

"Dad, I'm practically melting back here. The lake sounds like a great idea," Geri said.

Indian Head Pond was an immense lake by New Jersey standards. The bottom was sandy, the water a sparkly clear blue-green. Standing chest-high in the pond, I could see my toes wiggle.

The children loved it, especially Geri and Peter. By late afternoon they had to be practically dragged out of the water.

As I lay on the beach reading, Alyce screamed from the water, "Pete, look at Joe."

A group of massive boulders was close to the water's edge. Joe had climbed to the top of the highest boulder. Perched some twenty feet above the water, he stood beating his chest and making Tarzan noises.

“Joe, don't move from there,” I shouted. “I’m coming up."

I quickly scaled the jagged rocks. The sharp granite edges cut into the soles of my feet. There were gaping crevices between the boulders, and I shuddered to think what might have happened if Joe had lost his footing.

He started to ease himself down. "Don’t move. Just stay where you are."

It took several minutes to get down, picking our way carefully along the easiest path. At the bottom, Alyce rushed to Joe and threw her arms around him. "That was not a smart thing to do. If you had slipped, you could have gotten seriously injured."

My knees quivered as I imagined Joe atop the rocks, beating his chest. *Dear God, get us through this vacation in one piece.*

That evening at the campsite, Alyce stood at the trailer sink, banging on the faucet. "I can't get any water out of this thing."

I checked under the sink cabinet to ensure one of the children hadn't been playing with the cut-off valve. The water pressure gauge measured less than five pounds. I recalled the salesman saying the pressure should be maintained between ten and twenty pounds. There was a nipple on the water tank like the kind on a car tire. The salesman had said regular gas station compressed air could be used to recharge the water tank every three or four days.

"Pete, you've got to do something. We can’t wash or flush the toilet without water pressure."

"I'll have to drive the trailer to the nearest town to find a gas station."

Alyce and the younger children stayed at the campsite as Geri, Pete, and I drove into town. There were plenty of stations, but none of them had compressed air. That seemed weird. In New Jersey, all the gas stations had outdoor hoses connected to compressed air tanks.

"Daddy, we're going to have to buy a pump," Geri said.

"I should've brought my bike pump," Pete said.

We couldn't find a bike shop that was still open. As we headed back to the campsite, I had an idea. "Don't worry, guys. I believe I can fix the problem."

I had brought along an aerosol can of compressed air used to fill a flat tire. It probably contained enough air to recharge the water tank since tire pressure was more than twenty pounds. When we returned to the campsite, I retrieved the can from the car trunk and attached it to the nozzle on the water tank. As the air from the can entered the tank, the pressure gauge registered 15 pounds. I disconnected the charging can. The faucet coughed and sputtered as the air cleared the lines, then came out just fine.

We had brought along cans of crushed tomatoes and plenty of pasta. To celebrate, we had spaghetti with home-made tomato sauce, everybody's favorite. As we sat to eat, Geri said, "Mommy, the food smells funny."

Alyce sniffed Geri's plate. "Pete, she's right. It's either the sauce or the spaghetti. There's a chemical smell."

I had tasted the sauce as Alyce was preparing it. It had tasted fine. "The compressed air from the can gave the water a funny taste. I'm sure it's okay to eat."

Alyce took one taste and walked to a cabinet for a can of tuna. "I'm making tuna sandwiches. Don't eat anymore, Pete. Why take a chance?" Alyce asked.

I was famished and had already eaten a few mouthfuls. I agreed. There was a strong aftertaste. We tossed out our dinner and ate the tuna sandwiches instead.

That night I sat on the edge of the bed. "God, I feel like throwing up."

"I know exactly how you feel," Alyce said." She jumped to her feet and retrieved the aerosol can from the garbage. She read the warning sign on the label. "My God, it says it contains a propellent that could be lethal if taken internally."

I rushed to the bathroom. I now had diarrhea and made it there just in time. I felt momentary relief from the violent cramping. Suddenly I had to vomit and didn't have time to pull up my pajamas as I bent over the bowel, my rear end stuck out in full view of the rest of the trailer. The noise had awakened the children, and soon their laughter drowned out my moans and retching sounds.

Alyce closed the bathroom door, "Daddy is sick," she said.

When I finally came out of the bathroom, she was dressed. "I'll unhitch the station wagon. I'm driving you to the emergency room." My private nurse was clearly in charge.

At the camp office, she called the local police, and in five minutes, our entire family was escorted to the local hospital emergency department. I rode in the police car as Alyce and the kids followed in the station wagon.

They made me drink a glass of charcoal mixed with water at the hospital. They gave me ipecac to make me throw up. They ran a tube almost the size of a garden hose down my throat and washed my stomach with gallons of water.

I followed that protocol many times with ER patients. I never thought it was such a big deal. God, it was awful.

The doctor said some aerosol propellant must have gotten into our water supply. "Do not use the water for drinking, cooking, or showering."

They took a chest x-ray, did some blood tests, and after about four hours, assured us everything was normal and that we could leave. It was already getting light when we got back to the trailer. Later that morning, the older children went off to play. Jon climbed onto my bed and started jumping up and down.

"Daddy is sick," Alyce said. But it was too late. I awakened. My throat ached from the stomach tube, and I still had the sickening taste of the propellent in my mouth. Jon pointed to my mouth and started to laugh. "What's so darn funny?"

Alyce got a face cloth and began to wash my mouth. "The charcoal left a black ring around your mouth."

Alyce sat on the side of the bed, holding my hand. Jon climbed onto her lap. "Pete, you look awful. Your eyes are sunken in. I think you're dehydrated."

We sat there silently as Jon slid from her lap and began banging against a cabinet door with one of my shoes.

"Pete, between the manure and the smell of the propellent, I have to vomit every time I come into the trailer. And now you're sick. I hate to tell you this, but we must have run out of propane gas. The refrigerator and stove aren't working.

I lay down and closed my eyes. I said in a half-whisper, "Let's go home."

We left that same morning. Alyce and Geri made sandwiches for the trip back, so we wouldn't have to stop for food. Alyce figured we could make it back by 11 that night.

We had forgotten to dump our waste tank with all that had happened over the past few days. It held about twenty gallons. It was probably half full of liquid and solid waste. To empty the tank, you had to connect a large plastic hose to a nozzle under the trailer.

I slept until about mid-afternoon. Alyce had been driving for over six hours. I rubbed the sleep from my eyes, “Let’s turn off at the next exit and get some food. I'm starved. And let's see if we can dump our waste at one of the gas stations.

Geri and Mark stayed in the car as we went into the store. Ten minutes later, as we left the store, I saw Mark sitting on the I-beam that connected the trailer to the car. He was turning his body from side to side like he was steering it. Alyce lifted him off the I-beam and brought him to the car. “Geri, you were supposed to watch Mark."

Geri's lower lip quivered. "He said he wanted to get a comic book from the trailer. I told him to come right back.”

"I'd better make sure he didn't unhook any of the wires,” I said.

It was a grey, misty day, and the children were quiet as the open countryside, and an occasional small town flashed by. Alyce finally broke the glum silence. "Pete, we still have vacation time left. Why not go to Cape May for a week? I'm sure we can find a nice place if we try."

All the children started to talk at once. Cape May was one of their favorite places. Joe said, "Yeah, let’s go to Cape May."

We approached a railroad crossing as we drove through the next small town. I came to a full stop to make sure nothing was coming. As the back wheels of the station wagon passed over the tracks, I heard a loud crunch. The station wagon stalled. I restarted the engine and tried to drive forward, but the car wouldn't budge. I left the car and found the trailer jack jammed against the train rail. The jackshaft was bent, and the hand crank wouldn't. I assumed Mark had lowered it a few inches. I hadn't noticed that when I checked the wiring.

The rear of the station wagon and the part of the trailer were still over the train tracks. I shouted to everyone to get out of the car. I opened the car trunk, grabbed the tire iron, and began banging on the trailer jack, trying to straighten it or knock it off the hitch. It gave a little, but I still couldn't work the hand crank. If I disconnected the car, we could drive ahead out of danger, but the trailer would still be straddling the track. That could derail an oncoming train.

I got back into the station wagon, backed up as far as possible, and pressed the accelerator to the floor. The station wagon and trailer lurched forward a few feet before the car stalled. The kids were all clapping and screaming as I inspected the damage to the trailer jack. It had snapped off, but the hitch was okay. I threw the remains of the jack into the car trunk. The rear of the trailer was still over the tracks. I thought or imagined I could hear the faint wail of a train whistle in the distance.

"We have to get out of here fast," I shouted. "Don't get in the car until I drive the trailer off the tracks.

I tried several times, but the car wouldn't start. I must have flooded the engine.

"My God, Pete, hurry up," Alyce shouted.

I waited a minute or two and retried. It started right up. I quickly drove the trailer beyond the train tracks. I sat for a few minutes. My heart rate slowed as the children and Alyce piled into the car. A train never did pass by as we waited. I must have imagined hearing that distant, frightening sound.

"If we were all killed, daddy would've blamed me," Geri said.

"It wasn't your fault, sweetheart," Alyce said. She turned to me, "Why do you think that happened, Pete?"

"Mark must have cranked down the jack just far enough for it to get caught on the train track."

The drive seemed endless as Alyce and I took turns behind the wheel. Every ten minutes, one of the children would ask when we would get home. It made the last hours seem interminable. Finally, by 1:00 AM, the children were all asleep. We drove past Somerville, N.J., just 15 minutes from home. I suddenly remembered that the trailer was overflowing with our accumulated waste. There was no way I would deliver the trailer to the dealer in that condition. I suddenly had an idea. Along that stretch of highway, there were storm sewers every few miles. I spotted one close to a street light.

"Alyce, I'm stopping here to dump that Rizzolo waste into a storm sewer."

"Is it okay to do that?" she asked.

“This is an emergency. And besides, the sewage treatment plant is just up the road a bit. And if we dump it on the side of the road, it will end up in the sewer drain anyway.”

"You know how to do that.?" She asked.

"Let's check the manual." I pulled over and turned on the car's overhead light. Alyce read the manual aloud.

Alyce and I went into the trailer, where I retrieved a length of flexible plastic pipe from under the kitchen sink.

"When I tell you I have the hose connected, open this valve under the sink. The water pressure will flush all the crapola right down the sewer."

I put one end of the pipe into the opening in the storm sewer. I grabbed the other end and crawled under the trailer. It was pitch black. I fumbled for several minutes but couldn't get the pipe threaded onto the nozzle. I began to thread it part way on. when Alyce, her hand poised on the drain valve, shouted, "Pete haven't you gotten that hooked up yet?"

"Yeah, almost."

I guess all she heard was *yeah,* because she opened the valve and the force of the tank’s contents, rushing through the opening, popped the pipe out of my hands. Gallons of refuse splashed onto the pavement. I shouted for her to turn off the valve, but Alyce had already exited the trailer. When I emerged

from under the trailer, her mouth dropped.

"Oh, Pete." She quickly ran back into the trailer and got a towel and broom. She proceeded to clean my face. We were both too stunned to speak. I now reeked of a combination of propellent and a blend of family waste.

I drove the trailer forward and swept the waste onto the shoulder and beyond onto the grass.

"Don't you dare bring that broom into the trailer, Alyce insisted.

I tossed it onto the grass.

As we pulled away, five-year-old Mark, asleep between us, awakened. He climbed onto Alyce's lap. Unaware of what had just happened, he said, "Daddy, this was the greatest vacation we ever had. I can't wait till next year."

*****

LIFE'S FINAL CHAPTER

(Based on a true story)

RJ looked east as the sun announced its coming…a crimson rim of light along the distant horizon. Rocking gently, he watched a field of alfalfa sway in the early summer breeze. Despite his wretchedly poor vision, he could see his wife still in her nightgown, gathering wildflowers and his sons Robbie and Jessie tumbling in the grass. The scene dimmed and receded into the inner world of memory. The flu epidemic took from him his wife, Emma, and Jessie. Years later, his son Robbie joined the army after the Japanese attacked Pearl Harbor. He fought in North Africa and Italy. RJ was proud of his son and never permitted himself to believe he'd never return home. His young wife was left with an infant son to raise on her own.

"Finish schooling Makala. I can look after Josh."

Makala embraced RJ. "Oh, Pop, I can't let you do that."

"Still got one good leg. Diabetes ain't killed me yet. I still got plenty of get-up-and-go."

Makala moved in with RJ and went to community college after graduating high school to earn a teaching degree. She and her son moved to a nearby town, where she was hired to teach fifth-grade students

Over the next twenty years, Josh spent weekends and summers with RJ. He loved helping his grandfather. At first, it was everyday farm chores; but as RJ's diabetes worsened, Josh became his grandfather's caregiver. Over the next several months, RJ had a series of small strokes and one that left him unable to speak and residual weakness in his right arm and leg. His eventual loss of bladder and bowel control, the inability to bathe or dress, and inability to walk or stand without help, became too much for his grandson to handle. He was admitted to a nursing home at age 82.

His grandson was distressed by his continued decline. RJ eventually did not recognize him and thought him to be an intruder. He could not bear to see him, an independent man, who had worked hard all his life, reduced to such a helpless state. He gradually stopped visiting him at the nursing home.

The nursing staff described RJ as a cranky, occasionally combative man who often threw food he did not like. But on rare occasions, he would reach for a caregiver's hand and gently hold it to his cheek.

Because of his incontinence, he was bathed each morning, his bedding changed, and dressed in his Sunday best. He wore his black, patent-leather shoes on his good foot and his below-the-knee prosthesis.

When a new physician assumed RJ's care, he had already been a patient at the NH for four years. He learned that RJ had not had any visitors over the past two years. There was very little information on his medical record about his history.

He had contractures of his right arm and leg. He was unable to sit up or stand unassisted. He remained bedridden except when a male nurse s aide lifted him onto a wheelchair, where he was restrained and brought to the solarium where he sat in a broad circle of patients who, like himself, were alert, others dozing.

Mental status testing was difficult because of his inability to speak. His response to yes or no questions was nonverbal, with a nod or head shake.

On physical exam, the doctor noted swelling and tenderness in his right great toe. He had no palpable peripheral pulses and only a weak pulse in the right groin. He was treated with warm soaks and oral antibiotics.

The infection in his toe continued to worsen, despite nursing care and oral antibiotics. A surgeon from a nearby hospital was asked to evaluate him, hoping a limited surgical procedure would suffice. The surgeon vehemently disagreed. He recommended below-the-knee amputation. He felt strongly that antibiotic treatment would be futile; without surgery, he would die of sepsis in weeks.

When his doctor discussed surgery with RJ, it was impossible to ascertain how much he understood. But he consistently answered no to the recommendation that he have his leg amputated. His physician was convinced RJ understood what was being proposed.

A psychiatrist was asked to help determine if, despite his severe dementia, he was capable of understanding that he would almost certainly die if he didn't have his leg amputated. She determined after further cognitive testing that, in her opinion, he was incapable of making a rational decision. And that the decision should be made in consultation with his grandson.

His doctor called RJ's grandson and described the difficulty in ascertaining RJ's wishes regarding surgery. He asked if he would be willing to come to the nursing home, visit his grandfather and then meet with him to discuss how we should proceed. Josh agreed to visit his grandfather and become involved in deciding on his care.

Josh looked to be in his early to mid-fifties; a tall handsome man, wearing a shirt emblazoned with the logo of a local car dealership where he worked as a customer representative.

"I was shocked when you called…thought my grandfather had died…I don't remember much of what you said."

"I'm afraid I handled that poorly. Let me explain RJ's condition and the choices we must make. The blood supply to his right lower leg is extremely poor, and gangrene in the great toe will most likely spread rapidly. A surgeon who saw him in consultation strongly recommends below-the-knee amputation.

"If we choose to operate, intravenous antibiotics would have to be administered for several weeks in **a** hospital, or he would have to be transferred to a skilled nursing facility. All the doctors agreed that medical treatment had a slim chance of success, and gangrene would continue to spread to involve his entire leg. It would be a painful process lasting several weeks, eventually causing him to die from blood poisoning.

"You can't just let him die if you are sure surgery will save his life.

"Don't you think your grandfather's wishes should be what guides us?"

"When I met with him, it was impossible to know if he understood that without surgery, he would die. He didn't even know who I was."

"I asked the nurses who interact with RJ daily what we should do. They were mixed. Some believed he should not be forced to have surgery. That even if successful, it would complicate his care. He would most likely have to be transferred to a skilled nursing facility, a traumatic event for the patient and the nursing staff. To us, he is family, one nurse said. This, in a sense, is his home.

“Other caregivers were shocked that we would consider doing nothing and letting him die even though he resisted nursing care and was at times combative.”

“How can you ask me to make a decision that the doctors and nurses can’t agree on.”

“Would you agree to spend time with his grandfather for the next few days to reacquaint with him. You may better understand what his life here is like and what course of action would be best for him.".

Josh took a leave of absence from work and spent several days at his grandfather’s bedside. They sat in silence most of the time, RJ eying him suspiciously. Because of swallowing problems, he was fed a mushy, unappetizing vegetable and protein meal prepared in a blender. He ate very little, clamping his mouth shut after a few spoonfuls. Ice cream, Jell-O, and chocolate pudding were his favorites, but he coughed, gagged and struggled to swallow even with those foods. His weight had gone from 150 to115 pounds over the past year.

He fought his trips to the solarium but, once there, dosed listening to music, occasionally tapping his foot to the rhythm. He came to view his grandson as an employee because he began to feed him and assist the nurses in his care. At times RJ let his grandson hold his hand. His grip was surprisingly firm.

His grandson changed his mind about surgery. He decided not to go against his grandfather's wishes. He would not consent to the operation.'

They treated him with intravenous antibiotics, and much to everyone's astonishment, the infection slowly resolved, although he lost his great toe.

His grandson visited him often, assisting overworked nursing staff in dressing and feeding RJ.

Six months later. RJ died in his sleep at the age of 87

EPILOGUE

Dr. Sherwin B. Nuland, the author of HOW WE DIE, wrote, "Death belongs to the dying and those who love them. Although the incursive havoc of disease may sully it, dying must not be permitted to be disrupted by well-meant exercises in futility." Often the most accomplished of specialists are the most convinced and unyielding believers in medicine's ability to meet and conquer the dying patient's pathologies.

Medical students and residents are challenged to develop a specific diagnosis that underlies the patient's complaints. The more obscure the diagnosis, the greater the sense of pride and recognition the student or practicing physician gains. Dr. Nuland speaks of this as the "riddle" Solving the riddle becomes part of a doctor's DNA. Primary care doctors and subspecialists often feel compelled to solve the riddle, too often utilizing invasive procedures when the results will not improve the quality of life or significantly extend it.

Medical training programs will have to prepare increasing numbers of graduates to care for the ever-growing number of elderly approaching the limits of their life expectancy. The issue is how they choose to die, not if they die.

Every adult should think about and discuss with family and loved ones how they feel about end-of-life interventions and consider appointing someone they trust to make medical decisions when they are no longer capable of doing so.

A CHRISTMAS REMEMBERED

I couldn't wait for Christmas; although it was only three weeks away, I thought it would never come. My sister, Geraldine, had asked me what I wanted for Christmas. She was the second oldest of my five sisters and was the first to land a real job at eighteen. She had gone to Saint Rose of Lima, a two-year business high school. Somehow mama had gotten an old Smith Corona typewriter, and I loved to watch Geraldine practice. Her hands were a blur as they flew over the keys, and I can still remember the crisp sound the metal made as it struck the paper. I would wait for the bell to sound as the carriage reached the end of the line and how in a flash, she would snap the carriage back to the starting position.

To practice her shorthand, she would listen to the radio and take down what they were saying by drawing funny squiggly lines that made no sense to me. But afterward, she would read back exactly what the person on the radio had said. I wasn't surprised when Miller Brass hired her as a secretary at $12.00 a week.

As a child, I didn't feel deprived, although looking back, it was a no-frills childhood. The great depression started when I was an infant, and throughout my childhood, most of our neighbors were poor. We usually got crayons, puzzles, cookies, and candies for Christmas, but things like roller skates, trains, erector sets, and bikes were out of the question. We didn't exchange presents on birthdays, but my mother would bake a cake or make zeppoles, and we would all sing happy birthday. If I didn't remind someone, it was my birthday; at times, it would be forgotten until a few days later. I remember wanting to tell someone, but I figured if they cared, they would remember.

A week after my ninth birthday, as we sat around the dinner table, my third oldest sister, Philomena, looked up from a book she had propped on her lap. She said, "Mama, we forgot Peter's birthday again." My mother looked at me and smiled. She explained that they only celebrated Saint's birthdays when she grew up in Italy. As she leaned forward, I noticed that her breasts rested on the blue checkered border of the white porcelain tabletop. Before she could speak, Anthony, my older brother, said, "Well, Mama, Peter goes to mass every morning and says he wants to be a priest. Maybe we'll have a saint in the family someday."

Everybody laughed, including me, and my ears grew warm and red as they did when I had everyone's attention. I said with a serious expression, "I think I smell zap poles, Mama."

My twelve-year-old sister, Frances, who was very hard of hearing, clapped her hands in agreement.

My mother laughed and came over and kissed me on the cheek. We walked into the kitchen, and I watched as she got a large black frying and placed it on our gas stove. As she poured oil into the pan, I got flour, sugar, and a sifter from the pantry. I loved watching my mother mix the sugar, baking powder, and flour. She never used a measuring cup for anything, but somehow everything she made seemed to turn out great.

She dropped globs of the dough in the hot oil, and soon they puffed into odd shapes that quickly turned a golden brown. She lifted them with a slotted spoon and placed them on a platter. I dusted them with confectionery sugar. Soon the plate was piled high with zap poles. The pile shrank fast as my brother and sisters crowded around for "a taste."

My sister Geraldine put her arm around my shoulder and said, "I'm sorry we forgot your birthday, Peter." Everyone said my sisters were pretty but that Geraldine was the prettiest. Her skin was clear and light like my mother's, her nose straight, and her eyes and hair the color of the chestnuts I liked to gather as I walked to school. She looked more like my mother than any of the children, which made her extra special.

"Christmas is just four weeks from now, and I want to get you something nice," Geraldine said.

I knew what I wanted, but I was afraid to ask because it cost a lot of money. "I want to be a ventriloquist like Edgar Bergan."

She didn't have to ask what I meant because Charlie McCarthy and Edgar Bergan was the most popular radio show, and we listened to it every week. Charlie was a dummy whose mouth and eyes could be moved by manipulating strings at the back of his neck. He was supposed to be around 12 years old, and I was never sure whether Edgar Bergan was supposed to be his father, older brother, or just a friend. I guess you would call Charlie's humor witty, and as I listened to people talk, I would always wonder what Charlie would say.

"I'm going shopping at Bamberger's this Saturday. Do you want to come with me?" Geraldine said.

We took the number twenty-nine bus on South Orange Avenue and got off on Market Street right in front of Bamberger's. We took the escalator to the fifth floor. I discovered that if I twisted the rubber hand railing that moved along with the steps, I could get it to stop for a second or two. I did it when Geraldine looked at the Christmas list she had taken from her purse.

A lady ahead of us screamed and fell backward into a man standing in front of us. We were lucky she was only halfway to the bottom because it took two people to lift her before she reached the bottom step. I guess nobody noticed that I had caused the handrail to stop. Geraldine gave me a funny look when I told her it was my fault the lady fell over. I'm not sure she believed me.

The store was crowded with shoppers, and the vacuum tube they use to send messages from one department to another made a loud sound, like saying the word "soup" while at the same time sucking in your breath. When it reached its destination, a bell dinged at the counter where a salesperson waited on a customer.

The store was filled with the smell of pine trees, perfume, and new things. We walked to a counter in the toy department, and Geraldine asked a salesman if they had any Charlie McCarthy dummies. He took us to a glass counter, where four or five dummies were. They were different sizes and were not all dressed the same.

He pulled out a medium-sized Charlie, wearing a white felt cap, a blue blazer jacket with tiny gold buttons, and a red silk handkerchief in the left breast pocket. He wore a white shirt with mother of pearl buttons and a red bow tie. His sharply creased flannel pants rested gently on black patent leather shoes. His face looked exactly like the real Charlie McCarthy, with eyes made of glass that were almost scary; they seemed real. The fixed, wide-eyed expression was somewhere between a smile and a smirk.

"This is our most exquisite model, but it's our most expensive." He looked at us carefully and added, "We also have a very nice Charlie in our basement department."

Geraldine asked if I could try moving the dummies mouth, and after a slight hesitation, he said of course. I looked behind the head. There was a lever that controlled the eyes and a string with a ring to control the mouth. The salesman said you're supposed to rest the middle finger against the lever and place the index finger in the ring. I wasn't sure what he meant. Geraldine showed me how.

I rested the dummy on my arm and placed my other hand on the controls. Mustering my best Charlie imitation, I said, "Don't you think I'm cute? How can you resist me, babe?" I then rolled the eyes in a full circle like I had seen Edgar Bergan do many times. Geraldine laughed, and I noticed even our stuffy salesman had a nice expression on his face. He took Charlie from me and placed him carefully back in the case. He handed Geraldine a business card, "If you decide to buy one, please ask for me."

We went on to look at other things, and my sister never again mentioned Charlie McCarthy. My original high spirits began to fade as we wandered through the toy department and I became overwhelmed with everything I wished I had. The ball-bearing roller skates, whose wheels seemed like they would never stop spinning once I gave them a snap. A far cry from the learner skates my friends would let me borrow. We used to make scooters from old pairs of learner skates that people threw away. We'd remove a piece of hard rubber on the bottom of the skate so the wheels could move from side to side. Then nail the skate parts to a board. We nailed a piece of wood to the front of the board and an old broomstick across the top to make handlebars. The scooter would stop almost the instant you stopped pushing it unless you were going downhill, but it was still pretty much fun.

The smell and feel of the real leather baseball mitts were almost too much to bear. And the rows of wooden baseball bats stamped with black lettering that said, "Louisville Slugger," reminded me of the time I went to see the Newark Bears play at Ruppert stadium with my sister Philomena. On "ladies" night, she could get in for 15 cents, and I got in free because I was under twelve. We knew the names and batting averages of all the players. My favorite was George Sternwise, who played shortstop. I saw him get on first base with a walk and then steal second, third, and home. Everybody went crazy.

When we got home, I had a bad headache and told my mother because I knew what she would do. She asked me where it hurt, then lifted me onto her lap and began rubbing the spot with her thumb as she quietly said prayers in Italian. I didn't understand what she was saying, but after a few minutes, I would fall asleep, and the headache would be gone when I woke up.

Geraldine didn't realize I noticed the price of Charlie. It cost $8.99, almost a whole week's salary. She kept two dollars a week out of her check and gave my mother the rest. Out of that, she paid the bus fare to work and bought other stuff. It would take her a long time to save that much money. She did say she wanted to get me something special, but I knew I shouldn't count on such an expensive toy.

My three oldest sisters, Helen, Geraldine, and Philomena shared a bedroom. It was only one week before Christmas, and I couldn't stand it anymore. One afternoon when none of them were home, I sneaked into their room. I looked in the top three dresser drawers but didn't see a box big enough to hold Charlie. Finally, I pulled open the bottom drawer. Some clothes were spread over a cardboard box just about the right size. My heart was beating so loudly that I doubted if I would have heard anyone enter the room. I removed the lid, and there was something wrapped in tissue paper. Just then, my sister Helen shouted at me, "Peter, what are you doing in there?"

Helen said it was the worst thing to do, to spoil someone's Christmas surprise, and she would tell Geraldine, so she could bring back whatever it was she got for me. I burst into tears and said, "Please don't tell her. I swear, I didn't see anything."

That night as soon as Geraldine entered the door, Helen said, "I caught Peter snooping in the bottom dresser drawer. He says he didn't see anything but had that box open when I caught him."

I said, "I swear, I didn't see anything."

Geraldine took off her coat without saying a word and hung it in the hall closet. "I wish you had seen what was in the box because I don't want you to get your hopes up. There's no way I could afford to get you that Charlie."

I was sitting at the kitchen table doing a geography assignment. Without looking up, tears began to drip onto my homework. Geraldine came over and kissed my cheek. She said she probably would have done the same thing when she was little. She lifted my chin, so I had to look into her face.

"I didn't see anything, honest."

She hugged me and then began to talk about work. I liked to hear all about what happened at work because by now I knew a lot about her boss and the other workers. She said that last year everybody got a $5.00 bonus for Christmas and that this year they might get even more because they got a big government contract to make brass fittings for the Navy.

She said that they told her that when Philomena finishes at Saint Rose of Lima's next year, they would give her a job if she could type and take shorthand as well as her. She said that with mama sewing coats at home and her and Philomena working, we would be making enough money to begin saving to open our own business. Her latest idea was to buy a used bus and take people to Florida. The way she figured it, we could charge a lot less than Greyhound, make enough money to pay off the bus, and pretty soon buy a second bus. After a while, everybody forgot about Charlie but me, and I still felt like crying because I wasn't going to get Charlie.

Every Christmas, my mother threatened not to buy a Christmas tree because it was too expensive. And every year, late

Christmas eve, she would go out with Helen and Geraldine to find a place where they had leftover trees. She would offer them ten cents for the tree. They would laugh and say the cheapest tree costs $1.50 and that they would sell all their trees before midnight. Usually, they would come home with a beautiful tree by nine or ten. As we put the tree up and decorated it, we heard about how mama had haggled the price down to five cents. Helen would reenact the scene in Italian with English asides for us younger kids. My mother started very dignified, but as the evening wore on and they grew colder and more desperate, she described her other five children sitting at home in a cold flat with last year's tinsel poised to put on the tree that would never come. By this time, the man selling the trees gave up and told my mother to pick out one and to give him whatever she thought it was worth.

We had already cleared a place in the living room when they got home with the tree. Anthony had spread a white cloth and had set a big metal basin in the middle. They lifted the tree into the basin, and Anthony filled it with coals he had brought from the basement. I had some paper ornaments I had made at school. But my mother said it was too late for me to decorate the tree. I carried the wrapped presents and placed them on the sheet beside the tree. They were mostly things I had made at school. I gave the ornaments to Geraldine, and she promised to put them up front where everybody could see them. By this time, I was sleepy and didn't make much fuss about going to bed.

The following day, I awoke around six. At first, I thought nobody was up, but then I could hear my mother's and Helen's voices in the kitchen. They were talking quietly in Italian, and for an instant, I thought it was a Sunday morning, because those were the sounds, I heard every Sunday morning. Suddenly I realized it was Christmas morning and shot out of bed into the living room. My room was next to the kitchen, and I shared it with my brother Anthony. He was still sound asleep. Helen noticed me go into the living room and said, "Peter, don't open anything until everybody's up."

Propped up under the tree was a box wrapped in red paper. It was the same size as the box I had seen in the drawer. The tag said to Peter from Helen, Geraldine, Philomena, Anthony, Chickey, and Frances. I was sure they had filled it with old newspaper to fool me.

Every year somebody would get a big box with a bunch of smaller boxes inside it. And the smallest box would have something like a candy kiss in it.

I asked Helen, "Can we wake up everybody now."

She came into the living room and whispered, "They were up really late wrapping presents. I'll wake them around seven.

Frances, half asleep, came and sat next to me in front of the tree. We started playing a game of trying to guess what was in the boxes by the size and shape. When Helen left the room, we lifted the packages to feel how heavy they were. Then we shook the box to see what kind of noise it made. Boxes with clothes always felt light and didn't make any noise. Frances made a funny face when she picked up one of those boxes.

Slowly other family members gathered around the tree and my older brother Anthony as usual took charge. He found a present for each person and insisted we have just one person at a time open their present so everyone could enjoy the surprise. I kept looking at the red box and wished I could see right through it to the inside. I wondered why it had everybody's name on it. I must have been the only one there who didn't know what was in it.

When I finally opened the package, I couldn't believe there was the same Charlie McCarthy we had seen at Bamberger's. I looked at Geraldine and said, "But you said you couldn't afford it."

"I really couldn't afford it all by myself, so everyone chipped in, and we gave them five dollars down, and I'm going to give the store fifty cents a week until it's paid off."

Over the next few months, Charlie and I were inseparable, and I probably drove everybody crazy with the little routines I devised and made them listen to. My mother never really did understand my fascination with Charlie. I think she worried about her son playing with a doll, but Charlie wasn't just a toy. He was a friend. Charlie had a personality, a sense of humor, and wasn't shy. He would surprise even me with the things he would say. Through Charlie, I could be more me than I could as myself. I once brought him to school and did a routine for my class, and he was a big hit.

But as time passed, I got interested in sports and other stuff, and Charlie got put away in the same box I opened that Christmas morning.

THE BARN

Built on a base of stone, it rises
High above the frame farmhouse.
Eight by eight oak beam sills,
Joined to form its wooden base
More long than wide, its
Heavy posts reach as though in prayer.
Topped by sturdy plate beams,
Forming a lace of heartwood timbers,
Joined by hand-hewn mortice and tenon
And three stories above the ground
A roof of wood and steel sits confidently
Like the cover of a chest
Or the lid of a coffin.

A barn is meant to house the living,
A place of birth, nurturing, and growth.
A shield from wind, rain, and cold,
And at times, a playground,
A child jumping in oat bins,
Rolling in the hay,
And tying the cow's tails.
The stomping of started cows,
The laughter of a naughty youth.

But a coffin is such a quit place
Where young dreams fade and settle in dust
Where the building blocks of a man,
Break into a million tiny suns,
With orbiting planets waiting patiently
To be part of a living thing

Its sides, covered with inch-thick boards,
Grey with age, rough from countless rains and suns
and on the inside, pungent from dung and urine,
Of horses that had lived within those walls,
Their passing was not a time to mourn.
They lived lives of rhythm and purpose,
and were never promised more.
What do we tell the child once grown?
Why we sent him to a place far away,
For who knows why and at a cost too high?

The roof is not a straight line from crest to eve,
It has a hip running front to rear
On either side,
Like the wing of a bird,
Arched to better shield its young.
And what parent would not place their body
In the path of danger to save a child
From the rage of man?

Or a rain of steel cast by a faraway enemy
Its heavy doors press into the earth, locked ajar
Admit the wind to swirl and gather force.
To rile the smell and the sounds of old,
Of oats and hay and the sweet smell of milk still warm,
Of a child's scream and stomping of cows whose tails were tied.

Next to the stall of a loved first horse,
A folded flag rests upon the ground.
Its colors much too bright in this great space
Of browns and greys and night.

Anthology

Padre Pietro Rizzolo's

Pictorial Guide

to

Personal Peace

and

Professional Success

This edited collection of pre-digital B & W photography, rather crude images with appended whimsical musings, was prepared as a present to graduating Family Medicine residents. At the same time, the author was the director of their training program.

WE ALL NEED A MUSE

IF YOU LOOK CLOSELY, YOU CAN SEE MY ALTO EGO PADRE PIETRO BEHIND THE DOOR OF THE UNC GRAVLEY BUILDING (1982)

WHEN UNSURE WHICH PATH TO FOLLOW,
CONSULTATION IS THE WISEST CHOICE.
GOD IS THE ULTIMATE CONSULTANT FOR THE
FOLLOWING REASONS:
TWENTY-FOUR-HOUR ON-CALL SERVICE
HIGHLY EXPERIENCED
MAINTAINS STRICT CONFIDENTIALITY
ENABLES YOU TO BEAR THE HEAVIEST OF BURDENS
HE HELPS YOU TO WORK TOWARD YOUR
SOLUTIONS

FIND THE TIME TO PLAY
WHETHER IT'S JUST SITTING AND
WATCHING THE FLIGHT OF A BIRD

OR CELEBRATING YOUR IMPRESSIVE ATHLETIC PROWESS

OOPS! YOU MAY END UP IN THE DRINK
BUT NO SWEAT…INVITE IN A FRIEND
AND HAVE A LITTLE FUN.

WITH HARD WORK AND A LITTLE LUCK
WHO CAN SAY HOW FAR YOU MIGHT GO

DON'T BE AFRAID TO SAY, "HEY, WHAT DO I KNOW."
ADMISSION OF IGNORENCE
IS THE FIRST STEP TOWARD WISDOM

THE WORLD WOULD BE A DULL PLACE
IF EVERYONE WERE THE SAME.
BOTH PROFESSIONALLY AND
PERSONALLY, BE YOUR UNIQUE SELF
THERE IS GREATER RISK IN SUCH A
COURSE
BUT WITHOUT RISK, LIFE IS LIKE PIZZA
WITHOUT TOPPINGS

MAKE TIME FOR FAMILY AND FRIENDS
DO NOT BECOME DISTRACTED BY
CELEBRITY
AS YOU PURSUE YOUR CAREER

EXERCISE YOUR IMAGINATION.
IF NEGLECTED, IT WILL WITHER.
WHO CAN SAY HOW FAR IT WILL
TRANSPORT YOU?

May Day parade in Russia

I JUST JOKED ABOUT THE RUSSIAN
MILITARY
THEY WEREN'T AMUSED
HUMOR CAN OFTEN BE FOUND IN
UNEXPECTED PLACES
IF YOU LOOK FOR IT.
WHEN THE SEARCH BECOMES A HABIT
YOU WILL DEVELOP MORE CONTROL
OVER WHAT IS FUN AND WHAT IS
BORING.

EXPAND YOUR HORIZONS.
A LITTLE HELP FROM FRIENDS
CAN GO A LONG WAY

A VIRTUAL READING

The following presentation and reading presented during the Covid pandemic in 2021 explored memoir, memory, and legacy.

So many friends, former colleagues, and loved ones are all in one place, at least on my computer screen. It's a bit daunting. Stef Countryman is co-hosting this virtual event to keep me from messing up this amazing virtual technology.

In previous Q &A sessions, someone often asked what has contributed to my longevity and relatively good health. Of course, genetics and a long, happy marriage are high on the list, but luck and a passion for writing and tennis are not far behind.

Writing nurtures that mass of protoplasm between my ears and tennis the rest of my body. Passion is the driving force that gives one the get-up-and-go to pursue their dreams.

My tennis serve verges on the pathetic, it's speed rarely exceeding the driving limit in a school zone.

My ground strokes are just okay, but my determination to retrieve every ball hit to me as though my life depends on it, is my one redeeming talent, frustrating many younger and more skilled players.

A tennis buddy who is considerably younger than me often demands that he see my birth certificate. After enduring his chiding for too long, I admitted I had lied about my age and was much older, but I didn't want to make him and my other tennis partners feel bad.

****

For those of you who haven't read Besides Pasta /My early Years, I will summarize the prologue that introduced the memoir.

As volume one began, I was five, the youngest of seven children. My parents had separated in the early 1930s. My oldest sister, Helen, was sixteen.

The nation was in the midst of the Great Depression. My mother supported us with a part-time sewing job and a meager Relief check.

Rent consumed half of our monthly income, and the remainder never lasted until the month's end. We were not starving. My mother somehow managed to feed us, even the occasional beggar who came to our door.

She was a genius in the kitchen. Delicious meals materialized from food most people would throw away. She got vegetables and fruit on the edge of spoiling for free or bought for pennies. Soup bones could be had from the butcher for the asking. We ate free bread when she had the time to wait in the long lines for government supplies. We ate lots of homemade pasta.

Besides pasta, what we had in abundance was love for each other, a strong religious faith, dreams of a home of our own, and the belief that life with all of its suffering and loss was still pretty darn awesome.

Volume one concluded as I entered high school at St. Benedict's in Newark, New Jersey. Almost all of my teachers were Benedictine monks.

Volume two extends through high school, a year of day college at St. Peter's, evening college at Seton Hall, medical school at Creighton, internship, military service, residency, and the private practice of Family Medicine Flemington, NJ.

And the beginning of my academic career at a local hospital as head of their residency training program in the new primary care specialty called Family Medicine.

After forty-plus years as a doctor, my goal was to write novels that drew on my medical knowledge, experience, and interest in social issues.

I had listened to and reacted to tens of thousands of stories my patients shared with me. It was time to share some of my own.

Susan Sontag, essayist, and novelist, said, "For her, literature is a calling. It connects her with an enterprise thousands of years old. What do we have from the past…art, literature, philosophy, architecture? These are the things that last, sustain us, connect us to each other and history."

A memoir, unlike a biography, is not based on copious recorded data, historical detail, and annotated references. Memoir relies on the author's remembrances, landmark happenings, and relationships as they persist in memory.

It is a literary genre that has been around for a long time. Julius Caesar's first memoir, a commentary on the Gallic wars, was written over two thousand years ago.

Memoir is a kind of resurrection of life events of an individual. Happenings told through the unique perspective of the writer. Unfortunately, an individual's memories, unless recorded, slip into oblivion after one's death.

One's legacy is most often associated with the passing on of money, property, history of achievement, reputation, and culture.

Memoir, is an individual's or family's historical legacy, a valuable inheritance to our children and future generations. Without it, so much of our past fades and is forgotten. Letter writing in the past provided a valuable assist in the process of recall, but that has been lost, for the most part, replaced by ephemeral emails, tweets, and texting

As I wrote Besides Pasta Two during 2020, my brother and five sisters were no longer alive, no longer a phone call away to consult regarding events as they remembered them, context, or chronology.

Memories that are scattered among the billions of aging neurons that inhabit this aging brain did not pop up like a submerged cork.

I struggled to recall events that occurred decades ago and often failed, but at times did succeed in reviving seemingly inaccessible long-forgotten details. I have come to understand what William Faulkner said about the past. That the past never dies. It's not even past. As long as we are alive, it is part of who we are.

Even inaccessible memories are essential. They form a sub-conscious stratum that shapes what we like, fear, and cherish. How much of our preschool experiences can we recall in detail? Yet have you ever met a six-year-old child who doesn't know exactly what they like, dislike, love, or fear?

In writing part two of my memoir, I continue to use a narrative voice consistent with the period in my life I am recalling. I find that revisiting early life events more accurately evokes the excitement, joy, fear, and sadness I felt at the time.

We are not cameras that record our life on a memory chip. Human memory has tentacles. It is stored in numerous parts of our brain, making countless neuronal connections between life events.

Even when memory begins to fade, as it inevitably does, our most remote memories are the last to go, even in the face of cognitive loss associated with dementia.

Writing a memoir has been a virtual time travel that has been a three-year immersion into the past. It was a revelation as to the extent to which I was able to relive events and the associated emotions. I laughed, cried, and experienced joy, loss, sadness, and greater self-awareness.

It's an endeavor I highly recommend,

Here is a sample reading from this presentation:

At our first quarterly meeting in medical school, the president of our fraternity announced that he got an "unofficial call" from someone at the home office that a black student and one Jewish student didn't meet Phi Rho Sigma's *"traditional standards."* Code words for *Backs and Jews are not welcome in this fraternity*. He suggested that if we re-submit their membership application, leaving questions concerning their religion and race blank, they would be approved for inclusion.

Our president said our local branch welcomed all applicants regardless of race or religion, and he never endorsed such a policy to his knowledge. He was determined to retain the two students and was inclined to do as the home office asked. Two or three members agreed with the president, but most remained silent. I thought of my childhood best friend, Mark Stillman. How some of the kids called him, "that Jew-boy, friend of yours."

The Jewish student in question lived at the fraternity house. I did not know the black student, but I experienced racism in grade and high school in Newark, New Jersey. I was taught to love my neighbor as myself. One of my heroes was Dr. Martin Luther King.

I raised my hand. (a carryover from grade school with the Sisters of Charity). My caffeine tremor was back, made worse when I felt strongly about an issue.

"I don't agree," I said with a tremulous voice. "How can we humiliate our classmates by asking them to resubmit their applications? Tell me, what standards don't they meet?" I love this place and my new friends, but I'll leave if you do as they ask."

There was a long silence. Then three members of my study group stood and said they were opposed to doing as the home office asked. They didn't threaten to leave.

Our president agreed with the sentiment expressed but pointed out that if the Phi Rho Sigma home office rejected their applications, the medical school and university would certainly learn what happened. Our chapter might well be expelled from campus. We couldn't risk that.

A medical school senior and former president of our chapter said the main office was bluffing. They wouldn't dare risk the scandal that might follow.

Someone made a motion not to resubmit altered applications. The motion passed unanimously, and the main office relented and accepted their original applications.

Toward the end of my first year, I ran for fraternity's treasurer. I didn't have to campaign. No one else wanted the job. It involved keeping track of who paid and who didn't pay their room and board each month, paying fraternity dues, stocking the fridge with beer, collecting the ten cents the beer drinkers dropped into a kitty each time they grabbed a brew, paying our part-time cook, planning menus, paying the grocery and utility bills, and balancing our bank account each month.

The job covered my full room and board and a small monthly stipend. With what I still had in my savings account, I needed only five hundred dollars more to pay for year two at Creighton.

Oh, I forgot to mention an interesting fact about year one at Creighton: Cornelius Welch, the black student the Phi Rho Sigma home office said didn't meet their "standards," finished number one in the class. I'm sorry to say the Jewish student dropped out after the first year, although he did well academically. He never told even his closest friends why he left.

The Great Depression

A tall, middle-aged man in a worn woolen overcoat and crumpled fedora walked along the pavement, his form silhouetted by the light from a diner some distance ahead. He could hear someone walking not far behind him. A chill November drizzle gathered in the gunnels of his hat, dripping from the brim as he picked his way over the uneven slate sidewalk.

The footsteps grew louder, the pace increasing as the person drew up behind him. It was payday. His wallet, with two weeks' salary, was for the time being tucked safely in the inside breast pocket of his overcoat. The person behind him rammed a hard object into Eric's back.

"Hold it right there, mister, and don't try nothing."

Eric turned to face the hatless man. He was a head shorter than Eric. The man's right hand shook as he pressed the muzzle of a revolver into Eric's chest. His rain-soaked hair clung to his head and ears like a swim cap. His unshaven face was gaunt, his eyes wild with fear and desperation.

Eric's thoughts raced as he assessed the man before him. Probably in his early thirties, maybe younger. His slender hands were not those of a laborer, yet his speech was not that of an educated man. He wore an obviously once expensive but badly worn suit that hung loosely from his slender body. The man was shaking so badly that Eric feared it might fire accidentally.

"Please don't shoot a hole in my coat. It's all I've got to get me through the winter."

"You won't need no coat with a hole in your chest. Besides, you got a job. I saw you come out of the buldin' back there. Gimme your wallet."

"Why should I give you my money?" This man was no common criminal Eric thought.

"Are you stupid or something?" The man jammed his gun under Eric's chin.

The muscles in Eric's neck and back constricted violently. He could barely speak. "Let's talk about this. You want a cigarette?" Eric reached for the breast pocket of his shirt.

"Oh no, you don't. Keep your hands over your head."

Eric did as the man demanded. "You wouldn't shoot a man for five dollars."

"I'd shoot a man for a dollar, buddy."

"No. Not a man like you."

The man moved his face to within inches of Eric's "You know me from someplace?"

"No. But a man's face, his hands, his clothes, can tell you a lot about him. My guess you're a salesman of some kind. Maybe cars."

"Gimme you goddamn wallet. You don't know a thing about me."

"Let's go have a cup of coffee," Eric said. "We can get something to eat."

"What are you? A shrink or something" Rain dripped from the man's chin and nose. He moved away from Eric but continued to point the revolver at him.

"Take my hat," Eric said. "You're shivering. You'll get pneumonia." Eric placed his hat on the man's head. It dropped to his ears.

The man stared into Eric's eyes for several seconds. Neither spoke. He slowly lowered his right hand to his side. He didn't resist when Eric took the gun from him. Eric opened the chamber. There were no bullets. Eric placed the gun in his pocket.

"How'd you know it wasn't loaded?"

"I didn't."

The man slumped to the pavement. He drew his knees to his chest. "I can't even fuckin' rob somebody." He began to sob. Eric removed his overcoat and placed it over the man's shoulders, drawing it around his legs. He helped the young man to his feet. The pitiful condition of the young man moved Eric to suggest that he keep his overcoat.

The man looked incredulous.

"Nah. You said it was all you got."

"I have a job. I can always buy another."

The man grabbed Eric's hand and kissed it. He then turned and hurried off. Eric, coatless and shivering from the cold and rain, hurried toward the diner. As he entered, he suddenly remembered that his wallet was in his coat pocket. He rushed outside. The man was nowhere in sight.

Made in the USA
Middletown, DE
15 November 2022